A Dish Best S

Clay Cassidy

Edited and Published by Clay Cassidy

Also by Clay Cassidy

Payback
The Judge
The Return
The Serial Killer
A Dozen Lawmen
Wrong Diagnosis
Rebel Cowgirl
A Dish Best Served Cold

DEDICATION

I dedicate this novel to my wife Daleen and my son, Dean. They are the inspiration behind every step of me in the writing of this novel, as they realize that my passion for writing is to keep my readers intrigued and happy with what they read. Thank you for being my anchor when I was ready to throw in the towel several times before completing this novel.

TABLE OF CONTENTS

Prologue

It's still dark out when Jake rises, has a shave and dresses in his most casual, yet neat attire. He stares out of his Hotel room's window, enjoying the crisp, fresh morning air that holds the promise of a fine day.

As he looks down the dirt road leading into town, his thoughts involuntarily return to that fateful night in August almost five months ago. He was happily married then, his wife pregnant with their first child. That's now something of the past; something he doesn't need to be reminded of. What's done is done. The muscles along the side of Jake's jaw pull into a tight knot as he thinks about his wife and child.

CHAPTER ONE

The sun withdraws its last rays of sunlight when a rider becomes visible on the horizon. He sits astride a velvet-black Andalusia Gelding. The rider is dead-beat and bone-tired. He's been riding for six hours non-stop.

He packs twin six-shooters, one on either side. They are low-slung and within easy reach. The man is neatly dressed and wears a long brown trench coat over his denim trousers and long-sleeve cotton shirt. He combs the area with emerald-green eyes. His hair is long; touches his shirt collar and is thick and golden brown in color. His face is suntanned from spending long, hard hours in the saddle, and tight muscles outline his square jaw. He removes his War Bonnet to wipe the sweat off the inside of the brim, when a sudden whiff of wind ruffles his hair. It's a welcome relief, for the day has been long and sweltering hot.

His eyes scour the territory in front of him. Satisfied, Jake steers his mount in a South Westerly direction. He is eager to get himself a nice hot bath and dress in clean clothes after such a long, sweaty ride. He can feel by the way that Jet is galloping, that he too needs the rest, and some good barley and oats to eat. Jake pats his powerful neck while he talks soothingly to his horse.

"Not too long now, pardner. We'll be restin' pretty good in no time at all."

Jet whinnies loudly as if he understands, while he snorts through his nose and sways his head up and down. The wind plays with his thick, long mane.

About half an hour later Jake reins in on a low hill top, and in the distance he sees flickering lights. He steers Jet down the slope towards the sparkling town lights, where a hand-painted sign reads "Welcome to Bitter Creek." As Jake enters the town, he notices the Livery to his left, and immediately reins Jet in. An old man steps out and looks at Jet with big eyes.

"Mighty nice peace 'o horse flesh you got there, mister. Pretty big too, bigger'n I've ever seen!"

Jake nods his head and grins while he inquires "How much for the night, ol' timer? Give him a good scrub, and as much barley and oats as he'll eat."

"Gonna cost you one dollar twenty-five cents, mister. I'll throw in some special treatment, too.

Jake nods his head and replies "Yeah, that'll be good. What's your name, old timer?"

The man smiles and Jake notices that he has no teeth when he replies "Name's Gus. You wanna know anythin' goes on in this here town, you just ask me. I'll tell you."

Jake grins and thanks Gus.

"Thanks, Gus, I'll remember that."

Jake hands the old stable hand two five-dollar coins. He stares with wide eyes at the coins that Jake has given him, and then a wide smile covers his leathery, wrinkled old face. He can sure as hell save one of these for a rainy day!

Jake slings his saddlebags over his shoulder, turns away and walks down the main street in search of a Hotel where he can spend the night. As he walks, he looks at the other buildings surrounding him. There is the Black Jack Saloon to his right, and to his left, the Sheriff's office and town jail.

The lights are on in the Sheriffs front office. Jake guesses that the nightshift Deputy is busy doing his rounds in town. Then he is standing in front of the Hotel, which is an imposing building.

Jake opens the Hotel door and enters the lobby. A young girl comes out of the back office and greets him with a friendly smile.

"Good evening, sir. Is there anything I can help you with?"

Jake looks at her very fleetingly.

"I'd like a room for the night, please, miss, if you have any available."

Speaking to her forces him to look up and he can't help but notice that she is quite beautiful.

"Why, yes, sir. We do have rooms available. It's ten dollars a night, which includes breakfast tomorrow morning, a hot bath, and water to shave if you wish."

As she speaks, their eyes meet, and hold for a couple of seconds. She becomes a little flustered, and breaks the moment by pushing the register at Jake, who shows no sign of noticing her embarrassment. He takes up the pen she offers him and signs his name in the register.

"Is supper still available, miss?"

She regains her cool in the meantime.

"Yes, dinner carries on until eight o' clock. I will get the bell-boy to take your bags to your room."

Jake looks at his pocket-watch and is glad that dinner is until eight, because that gives him some time to take a hot bath and dress in clean clothes before he has dinner.

After taking a hot bath and dressing in clean clothes, Jake takes a seat at a table opposite an older couple in deep conversation. Jake guesses that the man could be in his early forties. He is tall with curly black hair, closely cropped and neatly styled. His wife looks friendly and at ease with herself, laughing every so often during the conversation.

Jake calls the waiter to place his order, After doing so, he is aware that the man looks in his direction, and then says something to his wife. She nods, and the man leans toward Jake.

"Evenin' stranger. Name's Buck Corbin an' this here's my wife Cassandra. I see you're sitting there all by your lonesome self,

Wondered if you wouldn't mind joining us at our table while we wait for

our supper. Come on over an' sit down."

Jake doesn't feel much like company, he doesn't have a lot to say lately, but then again; he can't dishonor the couple by not accepting their offer. Jake stands up, and walks around his table to the one opposite. He sticks out his hand.

"Howdy Buck. Pleased to make your acquaintance, ma'am", Jake says as he tips his hat toward Cassandra Corbin, and shakes Buck's hand.

"Name's Jake Hudson. Thank you for the invite."

Buck smiles and waits for Jake to seat himself before he says "Haven't seen you around here before, Jake. You just passing through or you thinking of buying up some land here about's? Coz I'll tell you, there's some prime beef country up for grabs here, and it's a steal at the price it's going for. Ain't no other land I'll let my cattle graze on, to tell you the truth."

"No Buck, I ain't from around here. Come from Wyoming. Just passin' through, like you say."

"You're a mighty long way from home, aren't you? Me and the missus have ourselves an outfit just a couple miles outside town. Call it the Grazing-C. Our youngest daughter works in the hotel here in town during the week, an' comes home on weekends. That's why we're here tonight, so Rhonda can go home with us

tomorrow afternoon."

While they're talking, their dinner arrives. It's Cassandra who breaks into Jake's thoughts while they are eating.

"I beg your pardon Jake, I don't want to pry into your personal life, and I know it's not my business. I noticed that you're wearing a wedding ring, so I suppose you're on your way home?"

Hearing these words, Jake feels the blood drain from his face, and he has to struggle to keep his composure. Both Buck and Cassandra immediately see the change in Jake's mood.

Jake forces a smile. He has no ill

feelings towards Cassandra. How should Cassandra have known not to ask a perfectly honest question? After all, his wedding ring is plain to see for everybody.

"Now Cassandra, please don't worry about it. I'm fine, really, I am."

After these reassuring words from Jake, both Buck and Cassandra are at ease in Jake's presence. Buck extends an invitation to Jake.

"Jake, would you accept an invitation to come out to the ranch with us tomorrow? You can stay and visit as long as you like. We'd like to have you as our guest, and it is Christmas, after all."

Jake looks across the table at the two people facing him. He enjoys their company, too, and feels that it will do him good to spend some time in the presence of everyday, honest people.

"Yeah, I think I would enjoy that, thank you Buck. I'll be glad to have someone other to talk to except my horse."

They all have a good laugh at the expense of Jet. Jake feels good. His dinner has been splendid and tasty. All he needs now is a drink before retiring to his bedroom. Jake excuses himself from the table and walks out the Hotel's front door, on his way in search of a saloon.

The saloon Jake decides on looks decent from the outside, and there is not so much noise inside. He enters a docile atmosphere. The room's lighting is dim, with the smell of stale tobacco hanging in the air. There are around a dozen or so men sitting around having drinks.

The barman nudges closer from where he is standing behind the counter.

"How'dy, friend. What'll it be? The hard liquor's not too expensive, an' my beers are the coldest in the County."

Jake nods his approval.

"Howdy. I believe I'll have myself one o' those beers o' yours, barkeep. Nothing to quench your thirst like a cold one."

The barman nods, understanding this stranger's statement, for it's hot in these parts, and drinking hard liquor only makes a man drunk. Fortunately, most of his regular customers aren't hard drinkers.

"Comin' up. That'll be two bits, mister", the barman says as he opens the beer and hands it to Jake over the counter. Jake pulls out a chair at the bar counter, and sits facing the batwing doors. He thinks about his visit to the ranch, and is surprised to find that he looks forward to it. He doesn't take much notice of the six men entering the saloon. He takes notice, however, when their rowdy laughter pulls him back to the present. One of the men, obviously the one with the authority in the group, gets up and walks across to the bar, tapping hard on the counter with his gun butt as he reaches it. He calls to the barman.

"Hey, Sid, why ain't ye' runnin' to help us? Want me to bash your head in? Don' let me come fetch you, ye'll be sorry!"

Sid looks flustered when he approaches the counter.

"Burt, I don't want no trouble tonight, okay? I'll serve whatever you want, but the moment you start causin' a ruckus here, I'm callin' the Sheriff to lock you up."

"Take it easy, Sid. We'll see you over tonight, since we're tired from the ride into town. But come tomorrow, we're goin' to have us a real party, an' you'll be makin' a lot o' dough. So don't complain afore ye' know what's hangin.'"

Jake orders another beer, and while Sid hands it to him over the counter, Jake asks "So, Sid, who is this arrogant man giving you such a hard time?"

Sid looks to see if anybody else is in the vicinity before he answers Jake.

"He's the ramrod of the Circle-R a couple miles outside o' town. Those fella's with him are his goons, all of them are cowpunchers for the same outfit. I'm glad his son, Eric, ain't here tonight, cos he's the one to watch out for. Eric's a real hellbender and spoilt rotten by his father, seeing that he's the only heir to the Circle-R."

Sid looks genuinely disgusted when he speaks of Garth Larson and his son, Eric. Jake takes a second long look at the group sitting at their table in the back, and knows without a doubt in his mind that they are real hard cases. Always on the lookout for trouble, and more eager than most to dish it out. Wishing the barkeep good luck until closing time, Jake finishes his beer and leaves the saloon, going back to the hotel.

CHAPTER TWO

An hour before dawn ...

Jake is already up and has a shave. He dresses in casual, yet neat attire. Staring in deep thought out of his Hotel room's window, Jake enjoys the crisp, fresh morning air that holds the promise of a fine day.

As he looks down the dirt road leading into town, his thoughts involuntarily return to that fateful night in August nearly five months ago. He was happily married then, his wife pregnant with their first child. That's now something of the past. No need dwelling on the past; what's done is done. The muscles along the side of Jake's jaw pull into a tight knot as he thinks about his wife and child.

Jake is jerked back to the here and now. He becomes aware that the sky has turned a light grey. Jake decides to have an early breakfast, but realizes that it's a little too early still. He checks his six-guns, testing the triggers and cylinders smooth working. Half an hour later Jake descends the stairs and enters the hotel restaurant. Down in the restaurant he spots a man lingering around two tables from where he is seated. The man looks over at Jake's table, an inquisitive frown on his forehead.

He stares back at the stranger. His suspicion becomes reality when the stranger pushes back his chair and walks over to Jake. His Sheriff's badge is polished, and shines brilliantly in the early morning sun. He takes a stand opposite Jake, and in a mild-mannered tone of voice, introduces himself.

"Morning, stranger. I'm Sheriff Roy Jackson. Noticed you last night, but didn't have the time to make your acquaintance. Saw you talking to Buck and Cassandra, and any friend of theirs is a friend of mine. Staying long, or just
passing through?"

The Sheriff is a tall man, about six foot four or five, and in the region of about two hundred and sixty pounds. Jake sums him up in an instant, seeing that he looks to be fair and honest, but not someone to mess with.

"Howdy, Sheriff; please, take a seat."

Jake indicates the chair and extends his hand in a gesture of greeting. The Sheriff pulls out the chair and sits down.

"Name's Jake Hudson. Yeah, just passin' through for now. Goin' out to visit Buck and his folk at their spread for the weekend before I hit the trail a-
gain."

"Well Jake, I'm pleased to make your acquaintance. Hope you enjoy your stay in our town, and hope to see you again soon."

Jake thanks Sheriff Jackson, and with this, they again shake hands and part ways. Jake walks over to the saloon and spends quite a while in the saloon talking to Sid. He then walks over to the General store and purchases a new pair of denim trousers and a couple of shirts. A pair of good-looking boots catches Jake's eye, and looking down at his own, he decides that it will be beneficial to his feet to buy them.

It's Friday, and all the ranchers are doing their last minute shopping for the weekend and Christmas. Being weekend also means that all the ranch hands in these parts will be arriving in town to drink and party their weeks' wages away. At exactly eleven fifty-five AM, Buck and Cassandra's buckboard comes rolling down the main street.

Buck waves at Jake when he stops the buckboard and says "Howdy Jake. How're you doing today? Hope you slept well an' had a good breakfast. Oh, and to add to our luck, here comes our Ronnie! Now you can meet the most beautiful girl in the

Northern hemisphere."

Buck walks towards his daughter and takes her suitcase from her, placing it on board the buckboard. He waits for his daughter to greet Cassandra first before he leads her by the hand to where Jake waits for them.

"Baby, this here's Jake Hudson, a friend of ours. Jake will be spending the weekend and Christmas on the ranch with us."

"Jake, this here's my pride an' joy; Ronnie."

Jake takes her small hand and feels that it's strong but firm. Their eyes meet for a few fleeting moments. She holds his stare, though. It is long enough for Jake to realize that he can get lost in there. Her eyes are the brightest blue. Full, voluptuous lips and a heart-shaped face with beautifully rounded cheekbones accentuate her features.

To finish it off, thick chestnut brown hair falls from her head to frame her face like a picture. From there it continues all the way down to her waist in beautiful, natural curls. Jake recognizes her from the previous evening when checking in at the Hotel, realizing that she was the clerk at the counter. He doesn't have more time to ponder this, as Buck helps her onto the buckboard. Buck announces to Jake that they will arrive

on the ranch at around lunchtime.

As they pass underneath two gigantic boulders arching almost half way across the trail, Buck pulls up the wagon, and indicates with his hand.

"Jake, you're looking at fifteen thousand acres of the best cattle-grazing country there is on this planet, my friend. I am proud to say that this here is my property."

Bucks' face has a look of peace and serenity on it when he speaks of his ranch. Jake looks as Buck shows with his hand extended in front of him. As far as the eye can see, there are rolling grasslands and hills, topped by cliffs whose fingers reach out to touch the skies. The ranch is situated in a valley, fenced in by the cliffs on right hand, and everything is a beautiful green as far as the eye can see.

"Now this is where I can find peace", Jake thinks as his gaze caresses the landscape, savoring the view that crosses before his eyes.

After their brief halt, they go on to ride for about another ten or fifteen minutes before Jake sees the road fork to the right. In front of him is the most beautiful, picturesque house surrounded by the greenest lawn Jake has ever seen. Adjoining the barn is a corral where Jake sees thorough -bred horses that are free to roam an exquisite piece of land cordo-

ned off.

As they approach the massive house, a short, stocky figure comes from what has to be the bunkhouse. The ranch-hands and foreman have their living quarters here. He calls over his shoulder, and five more men appear.

Jake is first to offer Ronnie a hand getting off the buckboard, and she accepts with a faint smile.

"Thank you, Mister Hudson."

Buck has in the meantime, gestured to the short, stocky fellow, and with a warm smile, he he greets the family.

"Buck, Cassandra, welcome back home!

Ronnie, this place hasn't been the same without you! Hell, you look good. Seems like life's treatin' you good? But then, so it should, too."

Buck speaks to the short, stocky man as he calls Jake closer.

"George, this here is Jake Hudson. He's our guest, and will be stayin' with us for a while. Jake, this is George Richards, an' he's the best Ramrod this side o' the Equator. Don't be fooled by his size."

Jake and George exchange a friendly handshake. George's grip is strong and firm, yet not overpoweringly so. The other ranch-hands are also introduced to Jake, and after all the greeting is done, Cassandra says "Well gentlemen, and lady, it's lunch time, so let's go inside and see what's to eat."

At these words, she takes Buck by the hand, and leading the way, everybody else follows suit, entering the house.

Once inside, Jake can't help but notice that the surroundings speak of wealth and very good taste, which he reckons will be Cassandra's department. Jake finds himself sniffing the air, and at the same time, touches his stomach. The smell is so wonderful and inviting, that he can't help saying "I'm as hungry as an Ox, and about ready to eat a horse. Whatever it is, it sure smells mighty good!"

Buck gestures to the men to follow him, and they enter a warm, cozy room, which Jake guesses has to be the family room. It is rich in trophies, and photo's on different occasions of Buck, Cassandra and Ronnie adorn the walls. Jake can also see that Buck enjoys hunting, as there are trophies of Buffalo-head, bearskins, and a variety of different types of Buck-species fixed against the walls.

Jake goes over to where Buck is standing at the bar, tending with extra care to the needs of the two woman in his life.

When asked what he would like to drink, Jake replies that an ice-cold beer will be perfect, as it is quite hot on the ranch. The conversation is light and the atmosphere relaxed, and for the next half hour or so they just enjoy one another's company.

At exactly one-thirty, a bell rings. Cassandra stands up.

"C'mon, let's go and have a bite to eat. Jake, I'm sure you will enjoy the lunch. There's Venison for tonight from an age-old recipe my grandmother taught me, and it has always been a winner. Bring your beer along; you're welcome to enjoy it further at the dinner table while eating."

The meal that is served for lunch time, is splendid. Jake finds himself asking for a second helping if there is any. Pushing back his plate, he lets go

of a loud belch.

"I beg your pardon, didn't mean to be disrespectful. It's just that the food was so delicious, I couldn't help myself. Cassandra, this was definitely a meal unequalled to anything I have previously eaten."

Cassandra suggests that they retire to the family room, where coffee will be served.

Situated in the wall closest to the bar, is a glass sliding door. Once opened, it gives way to an enormous porch, with very comfortable garden chairs. There 1s a huge oval-shaped table. Buck suggests they go and sit on the porch. Everybody finds this a welcome suggestion, and without any further ado, they follow Buck out on to the porch.

The afternoon is calm and peaceful, and the sun shines like a ball of fire. The sound of various insects and other small animals fill the air.

A DISH BEST SERVED COLD

The next morning Jake awakes at five thirty, and while he stands at the window, he watches the sunrise over the horizon, bathing the new day in its fiery fingers of light. He went to bed late, as did Ronnie. They took a stroll on the ranch, talking about this and that.

Jake is comfortable in her company, and it's obvious that she is in his. He laughs a lot, more than he has over the last couple of months. Ronnie talks carefree and without any misgivings. She is honest, good humored and has a great deal of spunk, which is infectious.

Jake enjoys Ronnie's company immense-ly. Both find that when time comes to retire to their rooms, they want to remain in each other's company for longer. They each keep their distance, knowing that the time is not yet right to start or pursue anything definite, yet secretly they long to do so.

Returning to his senses, Jake leaves his room in search of the family. There is already scurrying in the front and outside of the house. Jake walks outside and looks at the early hustle and bustle. Just then, Cassandra appears in the doorway, and seeing Jake, comes towards him. A smile lights up her pretty face, acknowledging his greeting.

"Morning Jake; slept well, I trust?

I've already spoken to Ronnie, and she says you two had an extraordinary pleasant evening, walkin' and talkin'. I'm glad that you're enjoying it here with us. Come along, and I'll whip up a storm of a breakfast for you. Buck and Ronnie are already waiting for us. I came out here to call you in."

With these words, she turns and leads the way back inside the house to the now familiar kitchen. A coffeepot is idling on the stovetop, and the aroma fills the entire room. As they enter the kitchen, both Buck and Ronnie cheerfully greet Jake.

Ronnie gets up and, walking over to the stove, pours Jake a large mug of cof-fee, topped off with fresh cream and sugar. Jake takes the mug of coffee given to him, and tests the heat of the liquid with the tip of his

15

tongue. Satisfied that he isn't going to be scarred for life, he empties the contents of the mug with a few gulps.

"Sorry folks, I was real thirsty."

Jake places the mug on the table, unaware that a white foam-ring has formed on his upper lip. It isn't until Ronnie points at his lip, and let's go of a chuckle, that he becomes aware of the somewhat wet feeling. Quickly he uses a napkin to wipe his mouth.

Their plates are placed in front of them, and breakfast has never looked better. While eating, Buck mentions that

he has to go to the far South

East corner of the ranch to check some fencing. He asks if Jake will be interested In accompanying him. Jake is taken by the idea of taking a ride out on the ranch and at the same time seeing the layout of this land.

It's been a long time since he's had the opportunity to just go horse-back riding for anything other than chasing after outlaws. They reach an agreement on the time that they will meet at the barn, from where they will set out, and finish their breakfast.

On their return to the ranch house, Jake and Buck each enjoy a beer on the porch. It's now nearly dusk, and the early evening is accompanied by a soft breeze rustling the leafs.

Ronnie appears to call them for dinner. They have coffee on the wide veranda after dinner. Jake and Buck each enjoy a thick cigar. When the two women join them on the veranda, Jake raises himself and stretching his frame, excuses himself.

"Well, I hope you'll excuse me; I'm 'bout to hit the sack. Had a busy day. Have a peaceful night, see you all tomorrow mornin'. Cassandra, thank you for a splendid supper."

Jake turns to where Ronnie is sitting next to him. He bends down and as she looks up, Jake bends down and plants a kiss on her cheek, letting his lips linger there for a moment.

"Good night, Ronnie. I hope you have a peaceful night's sleep. See you in the mornin.'"

Ronnie touches her cheek and turns scarlet-red, much to the amusement of her parents. Ronnie calmly puts her arms around Jake's neck before he can pull away, and kisses him on the lips.

"Goodnight Jake. Hope you sleep well, because I sure will."

Far below, Jake can see the ranch house and other outbuildings, carefully cocooned between the mountain cliffs. Ronnie's voice interrupts his thoughts.

"This is my most favorite spot in the whole wide world. It's so peaceful up here. Every time I come here, I'm reminded of the fact of how small we are compared to all these majestic surroundings. Yet we as people think that we're so powerful. It's beautiful, isn't it?"

"Yeah, it sure is mighty pretty up here. I can understand you feeling small and fragile, coz if one starts taking all of this in, it becomes too powerful to fathom. As a matter of fact, I'm sure a person could find complete solace here. I'm glad you came to show me the spot where you come to, to find inner peace. This tells me a lot about who you are, and that I had not been wrong about you."

Ronnie smiles at Jake, and her eyes are alight with happiness at these words. She knows at this moment that she did not wait in vain for her soul mate all these years. What saddens her a little though, is the fact that Jake is so hell-bent on avenging the death of his wife.

When raising the subject with her father, Buck tells her to leave it alone, and that it's a chapter in his life of which he alone can kill the demons. Cassandra also said that he can't be made to choose, because it will always hang over their heads, and that it's something that has to be sorted out. Ronnie accepts her parent's advice, and leaves it at that.

"C'mon, we'd better be getting back to the Ranch. It's already four 'o clock. I still have to help mom prepare dinner."

Together they turn their horses, and at a faster gallop than before, find their way back towards the ranch house.

CHAPTER THREE

J ake pushes Jet as hard as he will go, for he wants to cover as much ground as possible in the shortest time. Cassandra has packed enough food to last him for at least a week. If he rations better, he can probably stretch it for more than a week. The sun slowly rises in the East, stretching its yellow fingers to chase away the shadows of night.

Jake can already feel that the day is going to be another scorcher, so as long as it's still a little cool, he can give Jet free reins to run. As soon as the sun rises he'll have to rein in on Jet, otherwise he'll exhaust himself running in this heat for a prolonged period of time.

They're going in a North Westerly direction, towards Amarillo, Texas. It's known to be one of the more civilized towns, where law has found an anchor.

After riding for another twenty minutes, Jake pulls back on the reins, and Jet slows to an easy trot. Jake keeps Jet at this pace until they approach the crest of a hilltop. Here Jake halts and, deciding to take a rest, unhitches his saddle.

He's been in the saddle now for about three hours, and has made good time. Jake opens the saddlebag in which Cassandra has packed the rations. He decides on a can of corned meat with scrambled eggs, together with a couple of slices of homemade bread.

It can be washed down with a pot of coffee. He starts the fire and once it's ready, puts the pot of coffee on to simmer. Jake makes himself breakfast, and is satisfied with what he's managed to make. The food is tasteful, and he enjoys every last bit of it, as well as every last drop of coffee. Jet also finds some tasty sweet grass to feed on, and is once again keen to take to the trail. Jake cleans the hardware he's used and, extinguishing the fire, saddles up.

They head West ward once physically and internally replenished.

AMARILLO, NORTH WESTERN Texas.

A bunch of eleven men, ride side by side down the dirt road entering town. They look exactly what they are, dirty, unscrupulous, and looking to make trouble for anyone crossing paths with them. Tex Burrows is in the lead, and is without any doubt, the leader by choice. They were originally only six men. Then, as fate had wanted it, their paths cross with that of five other owl-hoots making their escape from jail.

The biggest outlaw in the other group of five men goes by the name of Justin Cooper. He is wanted for armed robbery, kidnapping and murder; a real hard case. Tex however, is an even match for him, notorious amongst his men and others who know him, for his hair-trigger temper and lust for violence. He has an even greater love for torture and is extremely dangerous with a six-gun, having perfected a lightning fast draw.

Although it's only seven o'clock in the morning, the streets are already bustling with people going about their business. It's not to be argued that this day will be hot, the sun releasing its wrath upon the earth yet one more day. Tex wipes away the sweat that forms on his brow with the sleeve of his once-clean shirt. The kerchief hanging around his neck is stiff and stained with old sweat, as are his clothes; but then, so

is the whole groups' clothing.

They're all in dire need of a bath, shave, and clean clothing, in that order. Although in need of all these necessities, Tex and his followers know that there's no way they can allow themselves these luxuries right off.

A DISH BEST SERVED COLD

Their funds are depleted. Their last meal was roughly one week ago. Since joining up with the other outlaws, they've had to ration their supplies amongst eleven, and not only six men. This exactly halves their supply of food. They have to get some funds, so Tex decides that a few rounds of Poker at the closest saloon will be perfect. They can play for booze as well as fill their pockets, and then spoil themselves with some luxury treatment.

Tex reins his horse in, in front of the Wild Horse Saloon, and the rest of the gang follow suit. They tether their horses to the pole next to the water troughs, allowing the animals to consume water for the first time in two days. It's such a sight to see eleven strangers enter the town and dismount at the same time, that most people look on in oblivious disbelief.

The ordinary townsfolk know trouble when they see it. One look at this bunch convinces them that it's only a question of what is going to happen when. Their stares are returned with looks of disinterest from the outlaws, hostility etched in their eyes, promising vengeance if confronted.

On the boardwalk, woman who pass by the saloon on their way to the hardware store, are suddenly and without warning, harassed. Tex and Justin take the lead with a vindictive attitude. There are surprised gasps of astonishment from onlookers, and squeals of bewilderment from the woman who are being harassed.

Never before has this happened on the streets of Amarillo, not even by the most hardened criminals living here. The other outlaws join in, and soon there is physical contact, the woman being touched and caressed in improper ways.

Their husbands intervene, or at least try to be of some help to protect the honor of their wives, but it's futile. The odds are eleven to three, and in no time at all the three men's bodies lie sprawled in the dirt road.

Blood is streaming from a multitude of open gashes in their faces and heads. Tex grabs one of the women and kisses her hard, forcing her lips apart in the process. He ignores her screams and wriggling to escape from his hold. Suddenly Tex screams in agony and pain, letting go of the woman. He sinks to his knees, touching his lower lip with his forefinger. His face contorts simultaneously with rage and uncontrollable pain.

The lady has brought her knee up and kicked Tex in his manhood with full force, and at the same time biting his lower lip. She tears out a piece of flesh, which she disgustedly spits out on the boardwalk. She steps back, but before she can make it off the boardwalk to rush to her husband, Tex rises off his knees with a grunt.

He catches hold of the woman's wrist. Pulling her closer, he slaps her so hard that her head whips back. She falls to the ground with a thud. Tex turns on his companions, who are all having a good laugh on his part, seeing as how he'd got whipped by a woman.

"Shut the hell up, all o' ye' yeller

bellies! I'm sick o' you fools! If one of you even as much as looks in my direction, so help me; I'll kick your asses so hard, you'll be tastin' shit for a year, ye' got me? Lonnie, now you go in this here saloon, an' see that ye' win me a stack o' money, an' if ye' even think of keepin' some o' the winnin's for yourself, think again! If you do, you're dead! I'm goin' to look for a quack to see if my lip can be sowed back on. I'll find ye' all back here in the saloon, an' don't do anythin' without my say-so. Justin, I'm puttin' you in charge 'till I get back, an' ye' better not foul up if you love your life."

With these words, Tex bends and picks up the piece of his lower lip on the boardwalk. Cussing under his breath, he

walks away in search of a Doctor.

"What you all gawkin' at, you fools! Ain't you ever seen real men alive an' breathin'? Go 'bout your business, before we decide to have us some more fun, an' this time 'round we won't be playing."

22

To emphasize his point, Justin threateningly draws his six-gun from its holster and points it at a bunch of townsfolk close by. They scatter like a school of fish fleeing from sharks, leaving behind shouts of victory. The ten men enter the Saloon, and to their surprise find no resistance from anybody present. Justin sends four of the townsmen packing, setting himself and three of his men down at the Poker table. He orders the barkeep to bring him a bottle of the best Whisky available, with four glasses and an ice bucket.

"Okay, you fools, let's get the game rollin'! Dealer, you'd better not deal me any losin' cards, or you'll end up losin' more'n your dough. Just in case, I'll send one of my men over to the funeral parlor to get you a pine-box. So, unless you wanna rest in pine, you had better deliver!"

The dealer, a well-dressed man in his mid-thirties, looks like he is going to say something, then thinks better of it. He just gives Justin a crooked smile. Justin is not at all impressed with this, and feels like bashing the man's skull in, but heeds Tex's warning not to start any trouble.

Even Justin rather obeys Tex's orders. The cards are dealt, and Lonnie, representing Tex until he returns, sighs an inner sigh of relief when he sees the hand he's been dealt. He will do Tex justice, and in light of this, Tex will be ever grateful to him, making him his right hand man. Lonnie wins the round without having to call for any cards, and takes one hundred and twenty dollars for winnings.

Tex returns about an hour later, his lip stitched back, but he behaves like a bear with a sore tooth. He is in the foulest mood any of them has ever seen him, cussing under his breath and talking to himself, sweating profusely. Tex's lip is swollen, and according to him, hurts like hell.

XXX

It's exactly three forty-five when Tex, Justin, Jack, John and Lonnie enter the bank separately, not to arise any suspicion amongst the tellers or townsfolk who are still inside the bank. Josh follows three minutes later. There are two citizens who are still being tended to, and Justin, Lonnie and Jack fall into the queue to be "helped". Tex and John are making up a conversation about nothing in particular. It's Tex's idea to do this, so they can look busy.

Tex can't believe their luck when both the customers leave the bank simultaneously. The clock on the bank's wall says nearly three fifty five, and time to make their move. Tex gives the signal by drawing his six-gun and coughing. Just then the bank manager comes out of his office and heads for the door, putting up the sign reading "Closed."

He realizes too late that he has made a mistake by coming out of his office before closing the vault. Tex and Justin see at the same time that the manager realizes his mistake. Justin grabs one arm, sticking his gun into the manager's mouth, and forces him back into his office. John points his gun at the bookkeeper, whose mouth has sagged open, his face chalk white. He won't even try and breathe, of this John is sure.

The tellers are also scared stiff under the wakeful eyes of Lonnie. Jack takes his position at the window as instructed, and quickly peers out into the street. Everything looks normal, and he also sees Slick and Pete standing by the horses, holding the reins loosely in their hands. He indicates a thumbs-up to Tex that nothing suspicious is going on outside. They are in the clear so far ...

Tex enters the vault, and is astonished at what he sees. Never in his life has Tex seen so many moneybags in one place. Four large burlap sacks with dollar signs on their sides are stacked on top of one another.

"What's this, old timer? Do you always
have so much money in your vault?"

The bank manager is in a state of shock, and he stammers when he answers Tex.

"Sir, take what you want; please just spare our lives. Today is the day we keep the payroll overnight, until Pinkerton Agency comes to collect it tomorrow. There's fifty thousand dollars in there; take it all. It's yours if you want it."

The bookkeeper nods his head in agreement while feeling sick, and about to die of hyperventilation.

"Thanks pops, we're goin' to take it all anyway, with or without your permission. I'm goin' to give you one hundred dollars as a bonus for keepin' this here stash o' money for us. It was real thoughtful of you."

"C'mon Tex, let's get goin', time's nearly up. If those Deputies come saunterin' back this way, we're stuck, an' we're gonna have to fight our way outta this mess. Let's just grab the loot and get!" Justin cautions.

Tex, realizing that Justin is right, indicates to Josh to lend Justin a hand in taking the bags. Tex also looks out the front window again, together with Jack and, seeing that all is clear, beckon to the men to go outside. The bank manager, bookkeeper and tellers have been tied up and gagged in the meantime by John. Everything is running smooth, and even Justin finds it hard to believe that Lady Luck is smiling down on them.

Their horses are waiting out front, and the town's people aren't paying any attention to the bank, so everything is going like clock-work. As these thoughts keep Tex's mind busy, he doesn't notice that the people in the street are suddenly gone. When he becomes aware that it has become too quiet, it's too late, for at that instant a voice rings out.

"Hey, Burrows! Yeah, that's right; I know who you are! We got you an' your amigo's surrounded. There ain't no way outta here for you except if you go through us! This here is Chief Deputy Clarkson speakin', an' I have a coupla Deputies with me. Oh yeah, by the way, your three men who were posted on the rooftops are safely tucked away in cells. Don't make any hasty movements, 'cos we're all extremely good shots. Oh yeah, wanna know how we knew about your plans? Why now, one o' them pretty ladies you entertained last night, came to tell us about it early this mornin'. The man she was with last night was so happy that he spilt his guts about the whole shebang."

Clarkson has just finished talking, when Lonnie decides that he's had enough, and goes for his gun. All hell breaks loose after this. Lonnie grabs his chest, and falls to the ground, blood spurting like a fountain from a hole the size of a silver dollar. Tex hears the crack of the rifle as the bullet smacks into Lonnie.

How could this have happened, after he had cautioned the men not to speak to anybody about their plans? This isn't supposed to have happened! As Tex looks up, he sees three Lawmen where Dave, Harvey, and Ortego are supposed to have been hiding out to keep watch and cover them.

Jack, who is the last to come out of the bank, levels his six-gun, the hammer already cocked, ready to let them have it. He is standing alongside Tex, when, the next instant, he grabs hold of Tex's shoulder to stay upright. He lets out a high-pitched wail, similar to the cry of a baby, and as Tex stares at Jack, he sees his eyes die, and the front of his chest turns into a bright crimson red.

Slick and Pete however, are there, holding the horses' reins. A bullet grazes Tex's fore arm, and he lets go of his gun, at the same time running for his horse, cursing loudly. With experienced skill, he jumps in the saddle. Josh has also managed to mount his horse, and is about to swing it around, when he is knocked from his saddle by a heavy-caliber bullet.

Slick runs to where Josh has fallen, and helping him mount again, mounts his own horse, leading Josh's horse by its reins. Bullets are buzzing around them, and Tex decides that it's not worth fighting against these odds. Without looking back, or heeding the safety of his colleagues, he races at high speed towards the outskirts of town. Justin and Pete are on his heels as he reaches the town limits. John is also breathing down their necks, clutching a moneybag and heads for open country, lashing their horses to force greater speed from them.

Slick and Josh are way behind the others, because Josh isn't able to stay in the saddle at a fast pace. John and Pete each carry a bag stuffed with money, as well as Josh, but after he is shot, he let go of his bag.

He bleeds profusely from his shoulder, struggling to sit upright in his saddle. His face is contorted with pain, and he grits on his teeth.

They're all aware of the fact that Josh is losing a lot of blood very fast, and if the wound isn't seared quickly, he will die of shock and blood loss. Time is of the essence now, and they can't afford to lose even five minutes on the trail. Both Tex and Justin know for sure that a Posse will be formed and will be chasing after them.

If they can get Josh to hold on for just another hour, they'll gain an enormous head start on their Posse. They can then afford to stop and pay some attention to Josh's wound. Until then, he'll have to hang in there, and hope and pray that he survives.

Forty-five minutes later, Josh slides

sideways in his saddle, and falls to the ground. He is white in the face, and sweating like a pig. When Tex speaks to him, his speech is slurred. Justin suggests that they light a fire, and get Josh's wound seared. After all, Josh is his cousin, and family has an obligation to look after one other. It will also stop infection from setting in, as well as lead poisoning.

But first, they'll have to knock Josh out cold, because the bullet has to come out first. They don't have anything to deaden the pain with. He'll have to bite a bullet.

Fortunately, it doesn't take much of an effort to knock Josh unconscious for

the procedure that follows.

Slick's Bowie knife is used to gouge out the bullet. It's lodged against the collarbone, and takes some pretty deep digging. The same knife is used to sear the sides of the wound and the artery that causes the excessive bleeding.

Josh is stable for the moment, but still not out of danger. He needs a lot of rest, and will there for have to double-up, riding with one of the other men. Josh has to be held upright, even though he's still unconscious. His arm is put in a self-made sling to support his shoulder, and the group of men once again hit the trail.

Before doing so, the bags are opened to see how much money is inside. Tell tale is the expression on Tex and his men's faces when realization sinks in. The bags are stuffed with newspaper and a couple of stones!

Tex draws the six-gun he's taken from Josh. Livid with rage, his eyes wide, Tex is foaming at the mouth. It seems that he is about to have a stroke, and also about to shoot anybody that as much as just calls out his name. Justin knows something has to be done, and very quick too. He talks softly, but with command.

"Tex, c'mon buddy, don't pull that trigger. You're gonna lead every man in that Posse straight to us. Right now they're still strugglin' to find our tracks, but you squeeze off a shot, an' they'll come a runnin' like a pack o' wolves. We can make it to Arizona, an' once we're there, I have a lot of friends where we can hide out, no questions asked. Once we cross the State line, they aint goin' to follow us no more, 'cos they don't have no jurisdiction in them other States. See what I mean? Besides, we gotta pull Josh through, he put his life on the line for us."

Hearing Justin's calm voice, and what he says, has a calming effect on Tex. He seems to return from time travel, blinks his eyes a couple of times, shakes his head. Then he looks astonished as he sees the gun in his hand.

Slowly he holsters his gun, and the old look of authority returns, giving him once again that steely glint in his eyes. Once again everybody present realizes how dangerous Tex is. They've seen how quick he is to go off of his rocker, without even being aware of it. Tex speaks slowly, punctuating each word.

"Yeah, sorry I lost it there for a while, but you know how I hate it when I'm double-crossed, guys. We been had, an' that by one of our own men! Never thought I'd live to see this day, it's the biggest disappointment of my life. I'm goin' to kill the punk that ratted us out, even though it was unknowingly. I warned each and every one o' you that our plans were not to leave the hotel room, did I not? And along comes Santa Claus to spoil Christmas for us! This could've set us up for a long time, long enough to disappear and be forgotten of. But it's fine, I'll get my chance to catch up, even if it takes me a couple o' years. The wheel turns for everyone."

Having said his peace since leaving Amarillo in such a hurry, Tex feels in control again, although his rage and hate hasn't subsided yet. In fact, it has only just begun, and the longer he is reminded of their misfortune, the better. That means that he can let his rage fester and grow until it's an evil demon in its own right.

They mount their horses, Josh riding double with Slick, as Slick has a full blood Mustang, which is more powerful than any of the other horses and can take the extra weight. They're once again six men, but not of their own doing. Two of their gang has been shot, while the other three are awaiting a circuit trial Judge for armed robbery.

Fortunately, none of them has shot one of the Deputies, nor did they have any money from the bank. Tex thinks that it's futile for the law to chase after them, and expresses his opinion about this to Justin and the others.

After riding without any rest for three hours, and seeing no sign of a Posse on their trail, Tex calls halt, suggesting that they make camp for the evening. The sun has already set, but it's not completely dark yet, so they can still make out the dim outlines of the territory around them.

Justin is now glad that Tex insisted on sending Pete to the grocery store beforehand to purchase rations, otherwise they would have been wasted with hunger out here. They will have to make an early start tomorrow morning in order to get across the State line into New Mexico, and with Josh still unconscious, it isn't going to be easy. Hopefully tonight's rest will prove satisfactory enough to get Josh back on the road to recovery.

After dinner, which is made over a low fire, covered by a makeshift roof of brush, the five men organize their saddles in a half-moon circle. Justin sees to it that Josh's bed is made right next to his own. They then make sure that their horses are safely tethered to tree branches, and safe for the rest of the evening.

The men hide their guns beneath their blankets, loaded and ready, just in case they are surprised by unwelcome visitors. Neither Tex, nor Justin or any of the remaining men will admit to it, but the tension runs high. Nerves are jittery as each man replays the scenes of the day in their imagination.

Tex's ego has suffered a severe blow after being caught in the act of committing his first crime while on the run from another lawman. He realizes how this day's happenings have now pushed him completely over the edge and in plain sight of the law.

Every lawman in the County will be on the lookout for the entire party of men, and not only him. They have to have a serious meeting to discuss their options, which are, considering the facts, very few.

"Justin, guys, we have to decide what we're goin' to do until the heat simmers down, or until the search party stops lookin' fer us. Fortunately for us, there ain't no Lawman that was shot today, so they can't pin any murder charges onus. Also, we'll have to lay low for quite some time, 'cause it's gonna take Josh here a helluva long time to recover from his wound. Justin, you said you had some connections in Arizona where we could hide out until everythin's cooled down. We're not gain' to be able to travel fast with Josh, nor will we be able to travel very far in one day. Unless we can hide out somewhere close by until Josh is ready to hold up for himself. Do any of you know where we might find such a place? We have a maximum of maybe two hours on the Posse, an' lucky for us, they won't search at night."

CHAPTER FOUR

Jake awakes a little later than usual, and looking at his pocket watch, Jake sees that it's already seven o'clock. Hurriedly he prepares a light breakfast, and washes it down with a pot of coffee.

Jake grins lopsidedly at himself. After breakfast and coffee, Jake ties his bedroll to his saddle, slides his Winchester carbine into its sheath, and kicks sand on the fire to kill the smoke and heat. He lets Jet find his own way back to the trail at a leisurely pace, and once on it, he sets Jet in a Northerly direction again, giving him free reins to run at his own pace.

By midday, Jet has covered quite a distance, and Jake can see and hear by his hard breathing that his horse is tired, and needs some rest. He pulls the reins tight. Jet slows down to a trot, and Jake pulls off the trail. He steers Jet toward a giant boulder where there's a lot of shade to be had. He sees to it that Jet has enough lush grass to eat of, and then fixes himself a large lunch.

Coffee is, for the moment, at the top of his list of beverages, seeing that there's nothing else close by to top it. By estimation, Jake reasons that, if Jet wants to, they'll be able to ride into Amarillo by dusk. That will make it twenty-two hours in the saddle since yesterday.

While he waits for the coffee to boil, Jake unsaddles Jet and rubs him down with grass. He enjoys this immensely, because the saddle makes his backache. The grass gets rid of all the salt that has gathered there while he sweated it out. Two hours after stopping for lunch, Jake is back in the saddle again.

Jet quivers with anticipation, knowing that it's time again to show his master what he is made of. He makes the earth fly by. By two thirty the sun is riding directly overhead, a glowing ball of fire, its wrath as deep as the bottomless sea. Jake pushes on in spite of the overwhelming heat, every so often taking his hat off to wipe his forehead with his kerchief.

Fortunately, he filled up his water canteens with water not long ago, and he stops every hour. He sips from one canteen, and taking off his hat, pours some water into it so Jet can drink. This takes care of the danger of dehydration.

It's later than usual when dusk falls

like a cloak out of the blue sky, enveloping the hemisphere in soft pastel colors of red, grey, yellow and orange but to mention a few. Jake is always struck in awe by the beauty of such greatness. It's like a window opening up to a complete different world, inviting anyone who dares accept the challenge, to travel into the unknown. Far off, Jake can see the tiny lights that will be those of Amarillo; flickering to him in seducing gesture to enter the pulse of life that awaits the traveler.

Jake's eyes fall on the high clock tower as he enters the city and rides down the main street towards the flickering sign that simply reads "Hotel and Restaurant." He sees that the time is 06:35PM, and silently congratulates Jet on making such good time. On another sign below this, an advertisement says that rooms are available for the evening, including bed and breakfast, for a mere ten dollars.

Jake dismounts in front of the Hotel, goes inside and walks straight to the reception desk. Here he finds a young man tending to the needs of the Hotel guests. The clerk excuses himself from the other group of people, and comes to the reception desk.

"Good evening sir, welcome to the Belvedere Hotel. How can I help you?"

Jake is tired and not in the mood for chit chat. He simply nods his head and says "I'd like a room, and then I'd like to get my horse stabled and fed."

XXX

Jake is up long before the break of dawn. He washes his face, and pulling the curtains aside, opens both windows to get a draught through the room. He feels as good as a new six pens, and the fresh morning air promises an intriguing day.

At six thirty Jake leaves the hotel, and walks along the boardwalk until he sees the sign on the opposite side of the street that reads "Sheriff's Office." It's about two blocks down the road from the Hotel. Jake finds the door to the office open, and goes inside. A large, well-built man in his early forties raises himself from the chair behind a huge desk, comes around it, and offers his hand to Jake.

"Howdy, name's Doug Harper, I'm Sheriff here in Amarillo. My Deputy saw you ride in last night; came and told me

straight away."

He sees the puzzled expression in Jake's eyes, and smiles broadly at Jake.

"Don't worry none. Jake, isn't it; Jake Hudson? Received a wire yesterday afternoon from the Sheriff in Bitter Creek. Told me you were headed this way, even gave me a description of you. I briefed my men to be on the lookout for you, and let me know when you've arrived. I'm glad to make your acquaintance, Jake. Call me Doug. Have a seat, let's talk."

During the introduction to each other, Jake and the Sheriff exchange a firm handshake, and Jake takes the chair offered to him.

"I'm rather glad Roy sent you that wire. Saves me a lot of time explaining to you who I am. You know what I mean. Well Doug, see, it's like this. This goes back a couple months."

Jake goes on to tell the Sheriff his reason for his journey, at last explaining why he is here.

"I know they were headed this way; been followin' their tracks. I'll give you a detailed description of the leader of these men. Goes by the name of Tex Burrows."

"Hold on there for a minute, Jake. Did you say Tex Burrows? Now ain't that a coincidence! Just short o' three weeks ago we had ourselves an armed bank robbery, an' you'll never guess who our robbers were. Yeah, I see you're getting the picture. None other than these fools you're lookin' for. Except, they weren't six, but eleven. Apparently they'd ganged up with another scoundrel called Justin Cooper, an escaped convict, an' four o' his men. Durin' the shoot-out that followed, we killed two of their men, an' captured three other. Right at this minute, those three men are sittin' in my jail cells, waitin' to be tried an' convicted."

This is excellent news to Jake, and he again experiences the feeling of hatred and rage that sweeps over him.

"Doug, d'you know their names, the
guy's that are awaiting trial, an' the others who were shot?"

Doug sees the change in Jake's eyes change to cold hatred while his face contorts with anger. As a husband and father, he can understand those feelings. He also knows that he can't do anything to try and stop Jake.

"Yeah, the guys who got killed during the robbery, are Lonnie and Jack, an' the men sitting in my cells, are Ortego Diaz, Dave an' Harvey. Would you like to talk to these scoundrels, an' hear what they have to say? Maybe you'll be able to obtain some info from them that we could use."

"I'd appreciate that, Doug. Do you
perhaps know whose men you're holding in the cells, or haven't they been very co-operative up to now?"

Doug, who has been leading the way out of the office through a door that leads to the holding cells at the back of the jail house, with Jake in tow, shakes his head.

"Naw, no luck there, Jake. Other than their names, they ain't told us nothin' else."

Once there, Jake is shown where the three men are being held, each in a separate cell. Jake looks inside the first two cells, but doesn't know the men from Adam. Then Jake comes to an abrupt standstill, his eyes fixed on the man in the last cell.

"I know you. You're one of Tex's men. Your other partner, Lonnie, was shot during the robbery. Fancy getting to see you again face to face behind bars, ain't it? Bet you didn't think the day'd come when you'd have to face me after what happened in Black Rock, 'eh Ortego?

The man cringes away from the steel bars and cowers in the corner of his cell.

"Jake, I ..., we ... "

Jake turns his Stetson around in his hands, looking the man squarely in the eyes.

"Stop yackin', Ortego! You really think I'm goin' to believe your lies? You'll say anythin' to save your hide. Know this; you'll pay for what you did, even if it's not by my hand. Also know this; if by some chance you do get out and our paths should cross, your life won't be worth a dime!

Jake turns his back on Ortego.

"Thanks Doug, I appreciate all you've done for me. Believe you me, when our paths cross, there ain't gonna be no mercy extended towards them fella's. I ain't got no beef with Justin Cooper or his cousin, but if they wanna side with Tex on this one, it's their funeral. You want me to hand over my fire-arms to you while I'm in town? I plan on stayin' over again tonight, an' I'm familiar with your town laws here. I'm not goin' to complain if you wanna keep 'em overnight."

"Naw, that's fine Jake. I know you ain't gonna make trouble in Amarillo. You ain't the kind that goes around lookin' for it. Besides, from one Lawman to another, I might even need your help if I'm in a tight spot, know what I mean? Join me at say, 'round eight tonight at the Red Dragon Saloon for a beer or two, eh. I'll let my Deputies know that I gave you the thumbs up to keep your guns, just in case they wanna get a bit cocky. You know how Deputies are. Always tryin' their best to impress the townsfolk, an' even more so, the Sheriff. Most o' the time they mean good, but actually do the wrong things for the right reasons."

Jake and Doug have a good laugh at the expense of the Deputies.

"Sounds good. I'll meet you there at eight. In the meantime, I have to go an' have some breakfast, an' then fill up my supplies from the hardware store for my trip to New Mexico. See you at the Saloon."

The two men part ways and Doug starts ten- ding to the paper work piled up on his desk. He wonders when the day will come that he'll be able to just sit back and relax in his chair behind his desk. Doug loves his job, just not the paper work so much.

He has often thought of giving this task to one of his younger Deputies to perform, and by golly, today is that day! It's time for him to only delegate from now on. Without any further ado, Doug signals to one of his Deputies to come to the office. Once there, Doug tells him to go and call the others for an urgent meeting.

Darkness still hangs like a cloak over the camping site, enveloping all movement against prying eyes. The fire has burnt out long ago, leaving only a heap of warm ashes. Tex is the first to rise, and impatiently shakes the others awake, handing out a kick here and there to some who don't react quick enough.

Obscene language rings out in the quiet early morning air from the men who receive a kick in the back, only to regret uttering such words after discovering who the abuser is. The night was restful and without any mishaps, making it possible for all of them to sleep peacefully, except for the two men who Tex placed out to guard the trail.

Josh is awake, although not fully alert yet. He still has a slight fever, and will have to ride with some help. When asked how his shoulder feels, he complains that it's throbbing, and burns like hell, making him feel a little weak.

Tex decides that his riding buddy will be Justin, seeing as how him and Josh are related.

It's Justin's duty to look after his kin. Justin utters obscenities under his breath, careful not to let Tex hear him. He isn't in the mood to act as his cousin's keeper. It will mean he'll have to share his saddle and horse with Josh, which will put extra strain on him as well as his horse, causing them to travel slower than the rest of the group.

"Why in hell did Josh have to get shot? That Sheriff should've captured him back in Amarillo. At least he would've been able te get proper treatment, an' he would've been outta the way", Justin mutters while he helps Josh fix bedroll.

Josh hears Justin's muttering, and looks at Justin when he hears these words, but he's too exhausted still to start an argument with his cousin. He also doesn't want to cause unnecessary trouble. He will sort it out with Justin himself when he's up to it. In the meantime, he will have to swallow the in-
insults flung at him.

37

He isn't afraid of Justin, and the latter is aware of this fact. It's only because he is weak and immobile at the moment, that Justin takes advantage of the circumstances. Another week or two will see him as fit as a fiddle, fit enough to confront Justin about this new attitude of his.

"Who does he think he is to wish such bad luck on his kin?," Josh thinks angrily through the grey mists of his groggy mind.

"Hey, get a move on, we ain't goin' on a holiday. We're runnin' from the law, an' if they catch up with us, they're gonna throw away the key! Do you understand the meanin' of that concept? Move it, move it, you sacks o' shit! I dunno why I have to be saddled up with the likes o' you useless goons! Ye can't do anythin' right. Do I always have to spoon-feed you? We gotta cover a lot o' miles today before noon, and it ain't goin' to be long before the sun rises. C'mon Slick, you're ridin' up front with me, seein' as how you know this here territory, an' the spot where that cave is you're braggin' about. I'm leavin' in five minutes, an' anyone who ain't saddled up and ready to go, stays behind. Like I said, it's gonna be with a bullet from my gun enterin' your thick skulls."

Tex is raging mad because he has to

delegate and organize, to try to get everything in order for the group.

The cloak of darkness quickly makes way for the first shades of grey. Even as Tex speaks, the sun rises from behind the horizon. It showers the fresh morning air with bright orange and yellow beams that stretch their long fingers to reach earth, and engulf man and beast in sweltering hot waves.

Tex leads the way out onto the trail, everybody in tow, for these men know that Tex will do good on his threat that he's made. After travelling for a couple of miles, Justin finds that he is finding it difficult to hold Josh upright in the saddle. Josh is slumping forward, so Justin can handle the reins with one hand

only, finding it hard to steer his horse.

"Tex, wait up! We have to take a rest for a while, twenty or thirty minutes at least, man. Josh's slumpin' in the saddle, an' he's damn heavy! I can't hold him anymore, my arms're achin', an' my horse is gettin' tired as well. It's nine forty five now, an' there ain't no sign of any Posse on our trail. I think we can afford to rest for a short while, just te get our strength back. We been travellin' for 'bout four hours non-stop. Slick, what you reckon, how far are we from that cave? 'Bout another two hours or so, eh?"

"Yeah, reckon that's 'bout right Justin. We're makin' good time, better'n I expected. We might even be there before
noon."

Tex looks at the men. They all look tired, and he can also do with a little rest.

"Ok, fine. Let's call halt for a while. John, you help Justin there with Josh. Lay him down in the shade, an' wipe his face with a cold cloth or somethin'. Pete, you an' Slick come help me to unsaddle them horses, so they can roam 'round for a while, an' feed on some grass."

After giving these orders, Tex holds his binoculars in front of his eyes, scouring the entire trail for miles behind them, letting his eyes linger, but neither finds, nor sees any clouds of dust that could indicate that someone is on their trail. He is satisfied that they are not being tailed.

"Justin, I want you to keep watching our trail with these binoculars while we're taking a rest up here. Keep watch, especially where there're large boulders and trees, 'cos that's where they're likely to hide, should they be on our trail. I've had a look, and for the moment, I'm satisfied that we're not being followed, but it could be that they're too far back to see. That's why I want you to keep an eye open, just in case some puff o' dust rises up down yonder. The rest o' you men, do everything you wanna do while we're taking this here rest. Once we're back on the trail, there'll be no stops until we reach our destination, no matter what the excuse. Someone can make us a quick pot o' coffee, if ye choose to have some, otherwise it can also wait 'til we're up in them mountains and inside the cave."

All the men join in and in no time they gather enough twigs and branches to build a fire. Soon the aroma of fresh coffee fills the air, boosting the men's morale a little. Their spirits are a little lighter and they don't look so tired. Tex realizes that he was unreasonably hard on the men.

After all, they've suffered the same hard-ships as he has up to now, and Tex knows that everybody in this gang of outlaws is afraid of contesting his ways. He suspects that's why he hasn't had any challenges from any member of the gang. He also knows that nobody will muster up the strength to challenge him, because everyone knows his speed with a six-gun, and how much it takes for him to draw it; nothing.

"John, when you've finished your coffee, go an' relieve Justin from his post, so he can come back an' have some coffee. An' remember to be vigilant, be on the look-out for anything that might be suspicious, from dust clouds to small specks that move on the trail. If your suspicions are aroused, give me a holler. However, I very much doubt that we're still bein' trailed."

"Sure boss, no problem. I'll be on the look-out for anything suspicious, an' nobody from down yonder will even know I'm watchin' 'em, if'n there are any followers, that is."

"Thanks John, appreciate it."

Ten minutes later Justin joins Tex, coffee in his hand. He speaks in a subdued whisper to Tex.

"Tex, I'm tellin' you now, if Josh don't recover real quick, I'd rather shoot him. I don't have the time, nor am I inclined, to nurse him back to health. I ain't no doctor. He knew what he was lettin' himself in for when he decided to ride with me. I ain't his keeper! He's gotta pull himself together pretty quick, he was shot in the shoulder, not in the gut. So, I wanna ask you, not in front o' the fella's; don't scold me if things with Josh don't turn out the waythey're s'posed to. I ain't takin' responsibility for what happens from now on."

Tex looks at the spot where Josh is lying in the shade of a tree, and thinks about what Justin has just said. He realizes that of all the men, Justin is the one that will speak his mind, not afraid of the outcome, for he is a near duplicate of Tex. Tex respects Justin's point of view, as well as his reasoning, and can see that the other men also feel that they are being held back. Josh is becoming a hindrance, and Tex agrees that he has to recover within the following two weeks.

"I agree, Justin, an' I ain't holdin' you responsible for anythin' that happens to Josh. He's grown, so if it's in his nature to hold out on us, do what you think is right. I'd do exactly the same if I were in your shoes. You have to give him a fightin' chance, though. It's only fair. After all; he is kin."

"I knew you'd understand, Tex. I'll give him a fightin' chance alright, but he'd better not mess up. We can't take the chance an' leave him behind alive, just in case he mouths off to somebody, or let's somethin' slip. The chances of him bein' caught by the law, is also good, 'cos all he knows how to do, is makin' trouble an' bein' a thief. If he ever gets caught by the law, he'll spill the whole can o' beans on us."

Tex calls for time up, and the horses are saddled again to resume the trip. This time Slick is ordered to take Josh on his Mustang Stallion. As it's a much more powerful horse, it can carry the double weight with ease. They swing off the trail, and proceed to ascend the low mountain slopes for almost two hours.

Looking back down the way they have come for the past two hours, Tex can see why hardly anybody knows about the cave. To come up the mountain this way, one has to suffer from insanity. He would never have come up here had he been alone, even if he knew about the cave, but alas, it's too late now to turn around. Slick says that the cave is just in front of them, anyway.

The path they're travelling on, is narrow, and in some places there's hardly any ground for the horses to step on, making them fidgety and causing their nostrils to flair in panic. Then, all of a sudden, as they round a bend in the path, it widens and forms a plateau. Slick calls halt, and, dismounting, declares that they've reached their destination. It's nice and green at this height, and no matter how Tex looks, he can't see any cave.

"What the hell you mean, we're here? There ain't no bloody cave, nor any entrance to one, as I see the picture around us! Looks to me like you took us on a wild goose chase. I'm of a mind to shoot you right where you stand!"

Both Justin and Slick laugh at this remark of Tex's. While snickering, Slick holds up his hand and points with his index finger.

"Whoa Tex, take it easy. Look behind those branches an' leaves. Told you it wasn't easily noticeable from the outside, an' we're standin' right in front of it! C'mon, take a look."

Tex dismounts, and walking up to the straight cliff-side, carefully pulls away the green shrubbery. He can't believe his eyes. In front of him he sees a gaping hole, and, as his eyes grow accustomed to the dark interior, Tex can see that it extends inwards quite some distance.

"Well men, seems like Slick here has led us to the promised land indeed. Good job, Slick. First of all, I think we oughta send someone in there to make a hellavu fire, so we can have enough light inside to see where we're goin an' what we're doin'. Once we've accomplished that, we can get Josh and the rest of our stuff inside, an' make ourselves at home for a little stay. John, you an' Pete scrape together some dry wood an' brush, get a fire goin'. Make it a big one, so there's enough light to lighten up this whole cave. We need to see what's goin' on inside. Okay, the rest o' you men, get the horses unsaddled; go on, get a move on! We gotta get this here camp settled before the sun sets, an' it's only a couple o' hours away! Justin, let's have a talk."

Tex and Justin walk off to one side, under scrutinizing stares of the other four men. Josh isn't interested in their jabbering, the only thing he wants to do, is sleep. Tex is aware that the four other members are watching them, but he couldn't care less.

He is the leader, and he will decide what their plan of action is from now on. He needs Justin's input, because Justin knows this territory very well. He also, according to him, has some people he knows around these parts.

"We'll have to make do with what we have for the moment, but it aint goin' to be for long; ten days maximum. By then Josh'll have te be up an' goin, else I'll see to it that he goes straight to his grave. We're movin' outta here come ten days. We can't afford to stay any longer'n that. I'm sure that Lawman back in Amarillo's goin' to wire all the other County Sheriffs, if only we knew who. Fortunately, he don't know anythin' 'bout where we're plannin' on goin'. That would've been a disaster, huh?"

Tex gives a chuckle.

"We're in New Mexico now, just crossed the border 'bout two hours ago. When we leave here, we'll have to get our hands on some cash, so I suggest we go to some small town, where it's doubtful there's any wiring services. Anyway, even if there is, Ortego wouldn't rat on me or his friends, so nobody knows where we're headed. That'll mean the Sheriff there doesn't know anythin' about us. Let's head on up to Fort Sumner on the Pecos River, lose ourselves for a day or two, get some cash and buy provisions. Then we can travel North to Los Alamos. From there we take the trail further in a Westerly direction, an' cross the County line into Arizona. Once we're there, we'll go to Tucson, and then further up North till we reach Phoenix. We might even go for the Grand Canyon. Now that's a place where we could really get lost."

Justin offers Tex a cigarette, which Justin hand rolls while waiting for Tex to finish. They both light up and inhale deeply of the strong tobacco. It's obvious that they enjoy the luxury of finishing a cigarette at leisure. Justin listens intently while Tex talks, nodding his head now and then. He can't say it better himself, and tells Tex so.

"Tex, I think you've said it, man. It's the only way we can go. We could also drop in on my friends, an' lie low there for a while. Eat their grub an' so on, you know; save our rations for the trail. My friends are a couple o' miles from the Arizona State crossing, so if it turns out bad, we can get into Arizona real quick, know what I'm sayin'? We ain't really bosom friends, just know 'em from prison. Real hard cases, an' always lookin' to score somethin' from somebody for free; like buzzards. Don't actually trust 'em, but I reckon they won't try an' slit our throats while we're sleepin.'"

"Okay, then it's settled. I'll tell the guys when everythin's been done, an' everyone's in a relaxed mood, that our original route ain't goin' to change."

The men spend the rest of the afternoon trying to make the cave as comfortable as possible with what little they have. Fortunately, the lighting is good, as each of them have a storm lantern, and enough paraffin amongst them to last until their stay is over.

There is enough wood in the vicinity of the cave outside to keep a fire constantly burning, not a huge bon-fire, just one big enough to keep the temperature inside the cave at approximately room temperature. Everybody's rations that they purchased are packed out, and meticulously the same amount for each person present is shared.

Nobody has more food to eat than the next one, thus avoiding tempers to flare up and start trouble amongst the men. This includes tobacco and liquor, as well as some other necessary items.

Josh drifts in and out of sleep. He's
still weak from blood loss, but it looks like he's regaining some of his color, and he has even had a mug of coffee a little earlier on. As soon as the rest of the gang sees that Josh is starting to look a little better, they all want to talk to him.

Josh indicates to Tex that he isn't up to it right at that minute. Tex tells the men to cut it short, saying that Josh needs a little more rest before he will be up to a conversation. The men say that they understand, and leave it at that, each returning to their own tasks. Most of them are busy cleaning and checking their guns and rifles, just, as Tex points out "In case we need to do some shootin'. You never know what tomorrow might bring to your doorstep."

These words of Tex, and the fact that they are now hiding out in a cave, accentuates the fact that Tex's words should be heeded.

THE COLD, CRISP MORNING air is pleasantly welcome compared to the stuffy heat of his Hotel room, Jake thinks as he rides silently down the main road leading out of Amarillo. Everybody is still asleep, except for the nightshift Deputy and the Hotel desk clerk.

Jake had a good nights' rest, and can't wait to reach Los Alamos, which, by quick calculation, should not take him more than three days' travelling to reach, if he doesn't encounter any problems along the trail. He's decided to

skip Fort Sumner.

He surmises that Tex and his gang will be long gone from there by the time that he reaches it. Jake reckons he has a better chance of catching up with them if he rides hard for the next couple of days, and only rests when absolutely necessary; like eating, and resting Jet at intervals.

Dawn creeps up on Jake like a thief, suddenly throwing bright orange light in his eyes, indicating that the sun intends to scorch everything living with its intense ferocious heat. Jake puts spurs to Jet, something he doesn't like doing, but he's in a hurry, and it calls for desperate measures. As if Jet understands his masters' predicament, he stretches his long legs, and for the next few hours the miles seem to disappear under the thunderous roar of Jets' hooves.

It's mid-morning when Jake first hears, then sees, the Pecos River about half a mile off. He pulls the reins in, and slowing down, Jake walks Jet to the edge of the embankment. Jet is breathing hard, muscles rippling from exhaustion, his body glistening with sweat.

Jake unsaddles Jet before doing anything else, rubbing him down with handfuls of coarse grass to wipe the sweat off his coat. Jet drinks thirstily from the river while Jake continues to rub him down. Jake decides to take a rest by the river before crossing it, making himself lunch while doing so. He quickly scrapes together some twigs lying around, lights the fire and cooks himself a good meal. Jake walks to the riverbank, and looking at the water, finds a spot where it flows slow enough for him to take a quick bath, and rinse the mornings' dirt and sweat off.

CHAPTER FIVE

Noon; Los Alamos.

The rider who enters town, has the appearance of a saddle-bum. His four-day old stubble-beard gives him a rather menacing look. His clothing is crusted with stale sweat and trail dust. His hair is stiff with sweat, and even his horse, which had to have been, once upon a time, a magnificent animal, is trail-dead and ready to drop.

The man slides out of the saddle, and for a moment there, it looks as if he sways on his feet, and has to grab hold of the stirrup to stay upright. Slowly he leads his horse to the drinking trough, dragging one foot before the other. When he reaches it, he lets go of the reins, and when the horse drops its head to drink, the trail-bum soaks his head underwater alongside his horse.

Los Alamos lies in the clutches of this oven hot, dusty day. Strangers here are an everyday occurrence, so hardly any notice is taken of the stranger who has just entered their town. Only one person pays attention.

Sheriff Luke Johnson makes it his per-

sonal duty to know who enters his town, and what they come to do there. He despises saddle bums, because according to his standards, they are nothing but a burden to society, living off the scraps of food that people kind-heartedly hand down to them.

He has no time for the weak, neither for outlaws who come to his town to hide out or cause trouble. He has steel-blue eyes, brown hair, and a ruggedly handsome face. His smile is deceiving, for he has perfect, ice-white teeth. Smiling at someone, or something, doesn't mean that he finds a situation laughable or intriguing.

The rider that has just entered his town, captures his imagination, but he knows better than to let it run away with him. He's burnt his fingers like that a few times, so naturally, he has now become a little more wary. What stands out like a sore thumb is the fact that this bum carries twin six-shooters, and not only does it look like he's quite handy with those guns, he also looks dangerously fast.

Unseen from his office window, from where he has a view of everybody entering and leaving town, his eyes squinting against the glare of the midday sun, he watches every move of the stranger. Although dirty and unshaven, the stranger has a proud stature, which puzzles Sheriff Johnson. He watches the man as the latter turns and enters the Hotel, carrying with him a Winchester Carbine and his saddlebags. Five minutes later the Hotel bell boy comes out, and, taking hold of the horse's reins, leads it towards the Livery next to the Hotel. The horse has also since recovered, and seems to have more spunk now.

Nonetheless, he will continue to keep an eye out for this new man who behaves so strangely, yet purposefully. With these thoughts still in his head, Sheriff Luke Johnson walks on over to the Hotel, entering the lobby and walking straight to the clerk behind the desk.

The clerk looks up and sees the Sheriff. He taps nervously on the counter with his pencil.

"Lemme see the register, Tommy. I wanna know who that gentleman is that just came in. And you'd better shut your trap, I ain't in the mood for your jawbonin'. J. Hudson; where've I heard that name before? It definitely rings a bell somewhere, and I'll figure it out somehow."

Luke Johnson turns on his heels and strides out into the sunlight.

JAKE MAKES A BEELINE for Los Alamos, riding as hard as he can, pushing Jet to his limits, only stopping now and then for the most essential needs. He really thought that both him and Jet took it too far, and weren't going to survive the ordeal, but thank goodness, they made it.

He's so tired, that he can sleep for a week, and this is also the first priority on his list, to get a room and sleep until he awakes. He will then pay attention to all the other things that have to be done.

The following morning Jake awakes at seven thirty. He slowly opens his eyes and sits upright on the bed, looking at his reflection in the mirror.

"I would've thrown my ass in jail if I'd been the Sheriff o' this town. Shit, I didn't think I looked this bad! No wonder the desk clerk was skeptical when I asked for a room. He sure as hell must've thought that I wouldn't be able to pay the bill. Luckily I could pay him in cash. I'd better get me a bath and clean clothes."

Jake has decided to grow a short beard, changing his appearance a little. Tex won't recognize him straight-off when they come face to face, thus giving Jake the advantage. Almost unfair, some people would say, but then, neither was his wife nor child given a fighting chance for survival.

Jake has a good breakfast. The last couple of days on the trail has been anything but good living. Now he has to see the Sheriff. Walking casually, Jake sets off towards the Sheriffs' office, and from a distance sees that the latter is sitting on the boardwalk in front of his office, smoking a cigarette. The Sheriff is so engrossed with his smoking, that he doesn't hear Jake approaching.

"Mornin', Sheriff."

Luke Johnson whips his head up, his body jerking sideways as he does so. The chair he is sitting on, almost topples over. His eyes grow wide with fright, and for a moment he is at a loss for words, then regains his composure.

"Well, howdy there, stranger. Saw you come in yesterday afternoon, an' wondered what you were doin' 'round these parts. It was you, wasn't it? Haven't seen you 'round here before. Where you from?"

Luke Johnson stands up and motions for Jake to follow him inside.

"Yeah, I know you saw me comin' in. Saw you leave the Hotel after I booked myself in." Jake says and offers his hand in greeting.

"I'm Jake Hudson, an' you must be Luke Johnson. It's good to finally meet you. I sent you the wire 'bout three weeks ago from Amarillo on that bunch of outlaws I'm tailin.'"

Recognition flashes over the Sheriffs features, and he looks a little ashamed.

"Oh, right, yeah. That's why the name sounded familiar to me yesterday. Just couldn't place it, but I knew I'd heard that name before. Glad to make your acquaintance, Jake. Concernin' those outlaws, they ain't been here yet. I've been keepin' my eyes an' ears peeled, ain't seen or heard nothin.' Fact is, they could still be on their way here, if they're still of a plan to come this here way. Didn't you maybe miss 'em on your way here? You coulda gone right past' em on the trail without seein' them."

"I s'pose you're right at that, but I was in such a hurry to get here, that I didn't actually pay attention. By the way, you saw the condition we were in when we got here. My first priority was to get here as soon as possible an' take care o' my horse. He's tough, but out there, he would've died on me had we stayed on the trail another day or two. It's my fault, cos I steered my horse off course, quite by accident. By the time I came to realize my mistake, it was too late. There were no rivers or lakes close to where we were ridin', so we ran out of water, an' then I started runnin' out of food about three days before we hit your town. We're here, and that's all that matters."

After talking with Luke Johnson for a while, Jake parts ways with the Sheriff and decides to have a beer. Stepping onto the boardwalk, he sees the figure exiting the saloon a fraction of a second too late, and collides with it. The other figure is also large of frame, and both Jake and the other man go sprawling on the deck.

Jake raises himself in the blink of an eye and comes upright. He offers his hand to the man who is still sitting on the boardwalk, clearly not happy with what has just happened. By the look on his face, Jake can see that this man is in a foul mood. This incident has probably pushed him over the edge. Jake hopes that there isn't going to be any trouble, because he didn't ram into the man on purpose. The man's next words obliterate any such misgivings of settling it peacefully.

"You blind or somethin'? There's a whole damn boardwalk to walk on, an' you choose to ram into me? Well, I ain't gonna tolerate any pushin' around, you hear me! I'm gonna knock your goddamn head off, you sack o' dirt!"

With these words, he slowly raises himself into a standing position, and bunches his fists. He's just as tall, yet not as large as Jake in build, with a short beard covering most of his face. His clothing also has a pungent odor emitting from it.

"I'm goin' to bash your skull in, mister! Who d'you think you are?"

Jake looks at the man circling him and

realizes that it won't be a fair fight. He reeks of alcohol.

"Look friend, I didn't mean to walk right into you. I have no quarrel with you. Let's each go our separate ways and avoid any further trouble."

The man is adamant and won't back off.

"Yellow, are you? Too scared to face a man? Well, I'll show you!"

Jake tries once more.

"I don't know you. Keep on makin' accusations like that and someone could really get hurt."

"You wanna know my name? Alright then; I'll tell you. My name's Slick Davenport!

You satisfied now?"

51

Jake's head comes up, and he feels the old anger return once again. He remembers the names of the other gang members riding with Tex's outfit, and this man is one of Justin Cooper's men. He is also, according to Harvey and Ortego Diaz, very dangerous, and lives for the rush brought by violence.

Jake throws aside all misgivings of a peaceful settling. He draws himself to his full height, looking straight into Slicks' eyes.

"Yeah? I'm Jake Hudson. You're a ways from your gang, ain't you? I'm sure you know who I am, coz I know who you are, so if you wanna go ahead with your hand you been dealt, I won't stop you. There's only one thing you didn't keep reckonin' with, I can't let you go back to Tex an' live to tell him that I'm waitin' on him an' the rest o' the crew here in Los Alamos, now can I? That would spoil the surprise, an' we can't let that happen."

When Slick hears Jake reveal his name, Slick feels the blood drain from his face, his eyes wide in terror, and he becomes aware that his hand has started twitching uncontrollably. He stops circling Jake, and is now rigid. The townsfolk who have witnessed all of this happening, clear a large area. They know what the inevitable outcome will be, as does Slick. He feels sick to his stomach, and wishes he can turn the clock back only five minutes.

He knows he is facing certain death here, no two ways about it. Maybe if he can catch his opponent off guard, he'll be able to outdraw him with a split second to spare. He decides to act instead of waiting for Jake to make the first move. Jake sees the change in Slick's eyes, and knows the moment has arrived ...

Nobody sees Jake draw, least of all Slick. His last thought is one of conviction; that he's the one who will be known to have gunned down Jake Hudson. Slick, gun already drawn and aimed at Jake, starts to snigger when the first bullet smashes into his upper right cheek, taking half of his face away on

impact.

A DISH BEST SERVED COLD

The second and third bullets hit him in his chest within millimeters of each other. Slick dies before he knows what hit him, his gun-hand going limp and lifeless. By the time the gunfire has died down, Jake is already bending over Slick's lifeless body.

Jake realizes that Slick being here, means that Tex and the rest of his gang can't be far off. He was most probably sent into town to scout and, finding everything in order in town, is to report back, where after the rest of them will enter town.

Sheriff Luke Johnson arrives on the scene, and hears from the bystanders what has happened. He comes towards Jake, a faint smile on his lips.

"Looks like lady luck has rolled the dice in your favor, my friend. You've won the first round. When this man doesn't return, my bet is they'll come looking for him. If they're stupid, they'll all come in at the same time, giving you the opportunity of a life time. I think you can lay back and relax now for at least a couple of days before they'll come looking for their friend."

Jake turns and parts the batwing doors to the saloon's entrance. Entering, Jake resumes drinking his beer. He orders another and finishes it before getting up and walking towards the doors to exit. A man enters the saloon and stops Jake.

"Hey amigo, there're a couple of mean-looking hombre's outside. They just rode in five minutes ago. Saw the man you killed lying in a box at the under-taker's, and say he's their friend; they wanna know who did it. Say they're gonna cut out the shooter's heart and feed it to the dogs. Said to come and give the message to the one responsible. Reckon you better go and find out what's up, and give them what they're here for."

The man doesn't wait for an answer, but turns around and leaves. Parting the saloon's doors, Jake steps out onto the boardwalk. The surprise at seeing who the men are, comes as such a shock, that Jake momentarily loses his cool.

"What the hell ...? How'd you ... ?"

53

Sitting astride their horses approximately ten feet away from Jake, is Ortego Diaz, Harvey and Dave. The looks on their faces are smug, but the sight of Jake has obviously shaken them as well. He is the last person they expected to run into. In fact, they planned on never crossing his path again.

Jake coming out of the saloon, must mean that he has to be the man who shot and killed Slick! Why didn't they make sure who the man was who killed their partner in crime? Now they have Jake of all people to deal with. Harvey takes his gun out of its holster, and aims it straight at Jake. It makes him a little less nervous of facing the ex-Lawman out in the open, for he can remember what Jake told them back in Amarillo when he paid them a visit in jail.

Jake comes over the initial shock, and is once again in control of himself. He looks Harvey squarely in the eye without even batting an eyelid.

"Why aren't you fella's in jail back in Amarillo? I have a notion that I'm not going to like your answer to that question, and I'm also thinkin' that you might have broken out. Correct?"

The three outlaws exchange quick glances at one another, taken back by this true accusation, as well as his accurate description of how things happened. The only thing he doesn't know, are the details. Then again, they can fill him in, no sweat. Harvey seems to be the spokes-person of these three members of the outlaw gang, for it's again him that speaks.

"You know Hudson, I'm startin' to get mighty fed-up an' upset with your attitude towards us. Yeah, sure we broke out. Did you really think we was goin' to sit an' rot in them jail cells until some Judge came around and sentenced us to a couple o' years in a Penitentiary? I ain't really as dumb as I look, an' I'm actually aggravated by the idea that you might think we're dumb-asses. I whipped that Chief Deputy, Clarkson, pretty damn good after actin' up with gettin' sick. He was dumb enough to buy the act, and opened the cell door before I let him have it. Had to kill him though, cause he just wouldn't give up. We had to steal horses to leave Amarillo, an' for that we had to kill four more men. So all you Lawmen are good for, is make us kill innocent bystanders. I sure as hell ain't gonna sit by idly an' wait for a prison sentence. Now you know, what you plan on doin' about it?"

Jake looks from Harvey to Diaz and Dave, and immediately sees the flaw in their operation. Diaz and Dave are so sure that Harvey has things under control, that they aren't paying very close attention. They're smiling at a bunch of young girls standing on the boardwalk a few feet away from Jake.

He realizes that this is his only chance to make use of the uncomfortable predicament he is in. Harvey, seeing Jake's glance shift, looks at exactly the same thing Jake has just observed. The moment Harvey looks away from Jake, he knows that he's made a fatal mistake. He should never have let his guard down on Jake.

As Harvey whips his head back to where Jake is standing, he finds the spot empty. Jake moves two steps to his right, putting Harvey right in front of him, and not hiding behind his horse. Harvey swings his gun-hand in this direction, when Jake's hand becomes a mere blur of movement, too quick for any human eye to follow. He gives Harvey a chance to level his gun before squeezing the trigger.

The bullet slams into Harvey's face, taking with it bone and flesh as it drills a hole through his head. It exits his skull and splatters brain matter onto Dave, who is sitting astride his horse next to the deceased. Harvey falls like a bag of potatoes from his saddle, spilling blood over the horse's rump as he falls backwards. Dave and Diaz are dazed with the speed at which the odds have changed. Their guns are out, but they're unsure what to shoot at. Jake is not visible to them. He's out of their field of vision.

"Diaz, Dave, over here, you low-life skunks!" Jake bellows as he appears from behind Harvey's horse; not more than a few feet away from Dave. The gunshots have frightened Dave's horse, and it rears up on its hind legs. Dave fires a shot, but misses. The bullet smacks into the dirt between Jake's feet, kicking up dust and small stones. Dave's second chance is Hell. Jake fires two shots almost simultaneously, each bullet finding its precise mark. The force of the bullets lift Dave from his saddle and throws him face down into the dirt.

Diaz fires off two shots, but they both go far out of range, one bullet killing Harvey's horse in the process, the other slamming into the sign above the saloon. Jake moves away from the crowd of onlookers that has formed during the shoot-out.

"Diaz, you spineless Jelly fish! After everything you said to me back in Amarillo, I really thought you'd change, but seems to me you're as bad to the core as the rest of them. Turn and face me, you yellow-bellied worm!"

Ortego Diaz slowly turns sideways to where Jake is standing, waiting. He knows his hour has come, and he regrets everything he's done wrong in his life up to now, but he also knows that it's too late now to say so to Jake Hudson. The only thing to do, is to go out like a man, and with this thought in his mind, he levels his gun.

On the verge of squeezing the trigger, he becomes aware of the dead weight of his legs, and then he hears the loud bang. The pain is sickening, and he can't think straight because of it. Looking up to where Jake stands, some fifteen or so paces away, his left hand tries to hold back the flow of blood. Ortego Diaz's eyes plead with Jake to finish him off.

Then he speaks incoherently, blood frothing on his lips. As he pleads "Please, I beg of you, finish me off. Don't let me suffer this way."

"You're gonna die like the dog you are, Diaz. Now you know what my wife felt like after you left her on the floor to die. Burn in Hell with your friends!"

Diaz turns a yellowish color. He tries to say something, but the words die in his throat as he coughs up a bright red stream of blood. Death covers his face, and with a last involuntary shudder, he falls forward on his face in the dirt. There is dead silence amongst the crowd of onlookers, then a soft murmur rises.

They are surprised by the ferocity and speed with which it has all happened. From the time when Jake was held at gunpoint, to when it's all over, maybe two or three minutes has elapsed. Sheriff Johnson appears from out of the crowd, he has seen the men enter town and was on his way to the saloon, when he witnessed the entire showdown. He shakes his head in disbelief as he comes to a standstill in front of Jake, looking for words and not finding them.

"I didn't start this fight. These are three other members of the same outlaw gang I've been chasing. They were jailed back down in Amarillo, but they've just told me that they had managed to escape after killing a Deputy and three more citizens."

"Yeah, I know. I just received a telegram from the Sheriff in Amarillo, warning me to be on the lookout for these men. They broke out four days ago. I'm just glad they never got the opportunity to cause trouble and maybe kill some of my citizens. It ain't no loss to the community, you killing them. I should actually thank you. You saved me the trouble of having to deal with them scum-

bags. C'mon, lemme buy you a drink."

XXX

Jake is aware that his head is a ball of throbbing pain. It seems to take over his whole existence for the moment, and he has difficulty opening his eyes when he tries to. Finally, he manages to open his eyes, but his vision isn't exactly as he imagines it should be. It's blurry, and his eyes are painful when he looks into the bright light outside.. He's in hell, and curses himself for being there. Worst of all, he can't remember getting to the Hotel and into his bed.

Well, that's water under the bridge. No use in trying to wrack his now dead brain over something so trivial. He will now concentrate on replenishing his health and strength, and first on his list is food. Once he's had something to eat, he will have a nice hot bath, followed by the bed calling his name. He has to be rested out tomorrow. Jake strokes over his throbbing head, and promises himself that he will never drink so profusely again.

Looking at the time on his watch, he sees that it's seven forty five pm. There's still enough time left to have dinner. Jake gets up from the bed, walks to the cupboard and takes out a clean shirt. The shirt he is wearing, smells of liquor, which means that he must've spilt some Whisky on it during his wild drinking session.

This is the first time in his entire life that he can remember getting so hung over, and he isn't at all proud of it. Jake washes his face and pulls a comb through his disheveled hair. He looks and feels a little better than fifteen minutes earlier, although still a little shaky.

Dinner is delicious, and Jake feels like a million dollars afterwards. He goes directly up to his room, takes a clean, crisp towel and a bar of soap, and heads for the bathroom at the end of the hallway. The bath is revitalizing, and after a couple of minutes of soaking in the water, Jake froths up some soap on his face, and shaves while sitting in the bathtub.

Feeling refreshed and sober, Jake heads back to his room, undoes the towel around his waist, locks the door, and pulls back the bed sheets. After getting into bed, Jake lights a cigarette and lies in the dark smoking, thinking of everything that has happened that day. Foremost in his mind is the fact that he will be coming face to face with Tex and the rest of the gang in the next couple of days. Jake is charged up, and ready for his confrontation with the men he's been hunting now for so long.

Finding resolution in the fact that he will at last be able to avenge his wife and son's deaths, and resume his life, he takes a last drag of the cigarette before putting it out. With a sigh of long awaited anticipation, Jake closes his eyes. Within a few minutes, the calm breathing speaks of deep, restful sleep.

Dusk, on the outskirts of Fort Sumner.

Six men, hungry and thirsty, sit their horses a quarter of a mile off on the outskirts of the town. As night begins to close in on the surrounding area, lights begin to go on. Within a short time, the flickering lights look like a large swarm of fireflies hovering in the night sky. Tex chooses to enter the town under the safety of darkness.

This makes it easier to slip unnoticed past inquisitive and prying eyes. On Tex's command, all six men start moving forward at a slow pace, keeping the reins tight on their horses. The journey here was long and tiring, both men and beasts needing some time off to replenish lost spirit and energy.

Money is a problem, for this is a luxury they haven't had in quite some time now. Tex expresses his concern about this to Justin, seeing as how they have to pay up front when they book a room for the night. Justin's comment to Tex is not to worry about a small, insignificant matter such as that. He'll fix things up at the Hotel. All Tex has to do, is leave him to speak to the Hotel desk clerk. Tex doesn't mind leaving this little task to Justin. The latter is a smooth talker as much as he is a charmer. Tex has been witness to quite a few women who have doted over Justin just by the way that he speaks.

Tex spurs his horse, and with renewed energy, his horse shoots forward to take the lead as they enter the main street of Fort Sumner. The street is filled with people, celebrating the arrival of weekend, a few drunks blasting away on their six-guns to add a little flavor to the festivities. Amidst all this going on, the bunch of outlaws aren't spotted as they pick their way through the crowd towards the Hotel.

Dismounting, the men tether their horses to a pole at the drinking trough, and enter the lobby. A few women look at them in disgust, and pulling up their noses, hastily walk out into the night. Justin wastes no time in speaking to the clerk, and when Tex sees the look of mistrust on the clerk's face, he fears the worst. Suddenly the clerk gives Justin an understanding smile, although smug, and holds out two key rings to Justin, nodding his head.

Justin turns, facing Tex. A huge smile covers his face from ear to ear.

"Told you 'twas easy as pie, didn't I? He even said we could have dinner in the dining hall, he'll just add it to the bill when we pay. If that ain't luck, I dunno what is! Dinner carries on till eight, so there ain't no time to waste. I'll wash up later."

Tex is amazed, not believing his ears. He can't believe that Justin has managed to pull it off. Tex sniggers, an almost smile appearing on his disfigured face, thinking what a clever con man Justin turns out to be. Josh, Slick, Pete and John are sharing one room, while Tex will have to share the other room with Justin.

This means that they are also going to have to share the same bed, something that doesn't sit well with Tex at all. Well, he'll have to be content with the way things are for tonight, but come tomorrow, he'll make another plan. Justin can damn well be sure of that.

Tex orders a round of beers while eating, which carries everybody's blessing. Dinner is over in a flash, and after ordering dessert, nobody can think of a better place to be than in bed. Tomorrow will be the day to plan their next move.

With dinner completed, Tex, Justin and the remaining four outlaw gang-members ascend the stairs to their rooms situated on the first floor.

"Okay guys, tomorrow's goin' to be a real busy day for us. So come mornin', all o' you come to my room for a meetin'. There're some things we need to discuss before we do anythin' else. If we're a little late for breakfast, we can always go get some grub elsewhere. It would give us the opportunity to have a look-see around without arousin' any suspicion. Be at our room by seven sharp. See you in the mornin.'"

CHAPTER SIX

Tex has been awake for the past two hours, and it's still dark outside. An eerie silence hangs over the town, giving it an almost ghostly feeling. There's not a single light burning in the whole town; even the Sheriffs office is dark. Tex looks at his watch for the umpteenth time, realizing that only a couple of minutes has passed since he last looked at the time.

It's now 04:45 AM, and as he looks at

Justin, Tex feels a stab of jealousy. It appears that Justin sleeps without any worries. Even though he's murdered three people, served some prison time for it, and in the process of escaping, killed a prison guard.

Tex knows that Justin doesn't have any conscience, and because of this, Tex is a little afraid of him, although he will never let Justin catch wind of it. He'll be a dead cat if anyone ever finds out, but fortunately Tex knows how to keep his pose.

Well, to hell with all of them. He's going to go and have a nice hot bath, and just lie back in the water and relax while he smokes a cigarette. Tex takes a clean towel, soap, and his shaving kit, being careful not to wake anybody on his way to the bathroom at the end of the hallway. For an hour, Tex soaks himself in very hot water, foaming up the soap.

While Tex enjoys his bath, Justin wakes up and gets dressed. He lights a cigarette and stares out the window at the still sleeping town. Justin wants to talk to Tex about their latest plans, but he knows that

Tex will flip his lid, and it will definitely endanger his life. Thus, he'll rather keep quiet and do as he is told.

Tex is becoming more dangerous and ruthless by the day. Justin isn't planning on staying with Tex's outfit much longer. With the Lawman from Black Rock on his trail, and who knows how many other people wishing to get hold of him, it's no longer a safe option to be seen or travelling with Tex. The time to part has come, but he'd have to do it without hurting Tex's feelings, otherwise Tex will make him pay for it. With his life!

Justin walks into a saloon and goes to stand next to a man at the bar counter. Without thinking twice, Justin starts a conversation with the man, who has a tin star pinned to his shirtfront.

"You're pretty far out o' your jurisdiction, ain't you? Who're you chasin' this far out? I beg your pardon for bein' so nosy. Don't mean to pry or nothin', but it's seldom that we get visitors from so far off. Just bein' neighborly, is all. Name's Josh. Josh Parker."

Justin sticks his hand in his pocket, and pulls it out empty. He makes a face.

"Darn it, now I've gone an' left my money with the missus in the store. Oh well, guess I'll have to make do with a glass o' water. Barkeep!"

"Don't be ridiculous, you can't quench your thirst with water in this heat! Get yourself a beer, I'm payin'!"

This comes from the man wearing the five point star pinned to his shirtfront. His voice is, strange enough, not loud and deafening as one will expect from such a large frame, but rather husky, yet perfectly clear.

"Well, hell, thank you, kind sir. This is the first time in I don't know how long, that I have to rely on the kindness of a stranger for somethin' to drink. You have no idea how much I appreciate your kind gesture. I'm utterly disgusted in myself, dunno what I was thinkin', leavin' my money with the missus an' all. I therefor insist that I buy you a couple of drinks tomorrow afternoon, to make up for all your trouble."

"Call me Allister, and it ain't no problem buyin' a fellow man a drink or two. Unfortunately, I'm going to have to take a raincheck on your offer to buy me a couple of drinks tomorrow. I'm on my way to visit some kinfolk of mine up in Santa Fe, so tomorrow morning before the first Rooster crows, I'll be on my way. Our paths will cross again someday, and then I'll hold you to your offer."

Justin finds this Sheriff actually good company, and is certain that if he had not been on the wrong side of the law, they could have become good friends. That's when it hits him like a brick wall. Sheriff Allister McNab was a prison guard at the same prison where Justin served some time of his sentence, but not on the same block.

He was a Lieutenant, and there was talk that he wasabout to resign. That had been three years ago, shortly before his jailbreak. The prison talk was true then; McNab resigned, and became a Sheriff, that's why the name was familiar to Justin.

Luckily, they never met face to face in prison. If they did, Justin knows that they wouldn't have been standing here drinking beer and having this conversation. He'd either be dead, or locked up in a jail cell here in Fort Sumner.

After another couple of beers, and a few good laughs at some drunk bar jokes, they part ways. Justin is slightly drunk, and feeling real good about himself and what he accomplished. Tex will be happy about the prospect of fulfilling his plans, and he'll give Justin credit for sticking his neck out that far.

Justin goes straight up to the room he shares with Tex, not bothering to knock before entering. When he walks through the doorway, he suddenly feels all the hair on his body stand upright, followed by goose bumps.

He hears the faint click of a gun-hammer that is pulled back, and then the cold steel of a muzzle pressing hard against the back of his skull. He is instantly sober, all alcohol drained out of his system by shock. Justin's left side of his face starts twitching uncontrollably; sweat running down his forehead and stinging his eyes. His

vision is blurred.

"You take another step, or even as much as bat an eyelid, and you're dead meat. I saw you revvin' it up with my enemy pretty nice! Seems you two are friends for life, the way I hear an' see it. What you been tellin' your new best friend, Justin? I bet you couldn't wait to blabber your mouth off, an' that he's now plannin' my ambush. Right? I was thinkin' of shootin' you the instant you walked through that door. You know what stopped me? The fact that I wanna know exactly what you two was talkin' 'bout. Oblige me by tellin' me what the hell you two had to say to each other for that long. I'm really quite interested in hearing what you have to say for yourself before I kill you, an' don't try an' bullshit me. I'll know straight off when you're lyin' to me. Understand? Now you can nod your head to show you understand. Undo your gun belt an' kick it towards me. Walk to the bed an' sit down with your hands on your knees. Any sudden moves an' you're history!"

Tex's voice is as cold and hard as steel, and Justin knows that he is less than a hair's width away from death. The room is filled with animosity, and it's all directed toward him.

"Tex, for Pete's sake man, none of what you seem to have heard, is true. I haven't been conniving with that Sheriff! I didn't even know that you two know each other! He bought me a couple o' drinks, sure, but that's it. I was thirsty and made him assume that I'd forgotten my money with my wife. Gave him a false name, of course, an' he fell for it hook, line an' sinker. Took pity on me an' offered to buy me a few drinks, which I accepted. C'mon, you know we don't have no cash to buy our own drinks, Tex! Good thing I did too, cos he told me he was on his way out tomorrow morning before the first Rooster crows. Says he's on his way to kinfolk in Santa Fe for a visit."

Tex stands looking at Justin a few feet away, sees the hurt expression on his face. It's funny, but Tex immediately knows that Justin is telling the truth. He feels bad about accusing Justin of conniving behind his back, but it's survival of the fittest out here, and if you let slip, it's a sure fact that you'll end up second.

"Thanks for clearin' that up for me, Justin. I believe you've just made my day with what you told me, an' also saved your own life in doin' so. The fact that you got plastered along the way, an' got him to pay for it; I like that. Serves him right, an' it's a bonus to you. Now, lemme give you some good advice to remember for future reference. Never in your life walk uninvited into a room when I'm the only person in it. When someone doesn't knock before they enter my room, I get the idea they wanna surprise me, an' I don't like surprises."

Tex picks Justin's gun-belt up off the floor, and tosses it close to him on the bed.

"No hard feelin's, I hope. Wouldn't like to have to look over my shoulder the whole time. I could develop a stiff neck doin' that. Just had to make sure things were still as they should be, an' the way we planned it. Happy to know that they are."

Justin sighs an inner sigh of relief, and thanks his lucky stars that things have turned out the way they did. Perhaps it's because Tex knows him a little better than he gives himself credit for. He is scared stiff, especially since he doesn't know how Tex is going to react to the story being told to him. Justin doesn't think that Tex is a bad person. He's made some bad decisions in the past, sure, but so does everyone else he knows.

There's no other way out now, so he carries on doing what he knows best, with the best in the business. Justin starts when Tex speaks again, so engrossed in his thoughts, that he doesn't hear him at first.

"What the hell's with you, Justin? I talk to you, an' you don't take no heed of what I'm sayin' to you! Might as well be talkin' to the walls, cos I reckon you're deafer'n them bricks in the wall. You oaf! You know what I'm gonna do? I aim to get even with that Lawman, McNab. He ain't leavin' this here town alive, not if I can help it. He humiliated me, made me eat dirt. I ain't very forgiving, as you very well know by now, an' I never, ever forget. You're gonna tell me where he's stayin'. I'm sure he got around to tellin' you that, right? If'n you don't know, go back an' find out. Then you come back here, an' tell me. Got that? Oh, and don't try any funny business, if it had crossed your mind to warn him of my visit."

Tex is on the edge. He pulls back the gun-hammer one notch, and rolls the cylinder of his six-gun slowly over the palm of his left hand, listening to it click every time it rolls. It's his most prized possession, well-oiled and clean as a whistle. It's menacing even in the
dim light of the room.

Justin can't believe his ears. Is Tex crazy, off his rocker?

"Tex, what you talkin' 'bout? You can't go 'round just shootin' people as you please. Nobody knows where we are at the moment. We're home free. Let's keep it that way. I don't wanna be runnin' from the Law again, an' I'm sure the guys feel the same way. We can settle somewhere's up North, start a new life where nobody knows any of us. You wanna throw that away for all of us, spoil our chances of survivin' the odds. Don't be hasty now, Tex. Think about what you're about to do, coz once you done it, you can't undo any of it."

Justin feels his heart pound in his throat, and he feels light-headed. A faint sweat breaks on his brows and upper lip.

Justin looks to where his six-gun is lying next to him within arm's reach, and with a sickening feeling realizes that, even if he is able to clear it from the holster, he will never stand a chance of outdrawing Tex. He sees that Tex follows his gaze, and realizing what his thoughts are, has a sadistic, laconic smile playing on his lips, pulling them back in a snarl. The scar on his lower lip, which has now healed completely, makes him look more cruel than usual.

Justin realizes that no matter what he says now, it won't make any difference in the way things are going to turn out for him, but he has to try, nonetheless.

"Tex, I..., I dunno what you're gettin' at by..."

"Shut your trap, Justin. I've had it with your jawbonin' an' actin'. I know, an' you know, what you were just thinkin', a moment ago. Well, if you wanna give it a shot, go right ahead. I'll give you enough time to clear leather before I kill you, cos now I know I can't trust you no more, so, no matter whether you try or not, you've had it. Thanks for keepin' me company for a while, but this is where our paths split. Only thing is, you're goin' to hell sooner than planned, an' way before me. Keep me a free entry ticket, will you? Just in case."

Tex thumbs back the hammer on his six-shooter, watching with delight as the fear jumps into Justin's eyes when realization sets in. Justin lunges for his gun, and in one smooth action pulls it from its holster, his thumb already pulling back the hammer.

Once the gun is clear from its holster, Justin spins around in half an upright position, bringing his right arm up to trigger a shot. Too late does he realize that Tex has changed the spot from his previous position. Horrorstricken, Justin starts turning to where his eye has caught a glimpse of movement. His last thought is one of a cold, sick, nauseating warmness in the pit of his stomach, only to realize that it's the first bullet burning a hole into his gut.

His gun-hand slips, faltering in its upright swing, and he catches himself clutching at his stomach, trying to scratch out the burning hurt that overwhelms him. The second bullet hits him square in the chest, throwing him over backwards, while a third bullet blows away the left side of his face. It's all over in less than five seconds. Justin dies on his feet with the impact of the second bullet smashing a hole in his chest cavity the size of a silver dollar coin.

There is shouting in the corridor outside his hotel room, and looking out the window, Tex sees the Sheriff and two of his Deputies run across from the Sheriff's office towards the Hotel, pulling out their handguns in the process. Tex realizes that he has to get out of the hotel, and be quick about it.

He'll be gunned down like a dog once the Law catches up with him, because he isn't considering giving up arms. The best way now is West, and getting there as soon as possible. Hiding out at Justin's friends is now out of the question as well, seeing as Tex doesn't know where they live. Then there's Josh to keep reckoning with. He is sure not to be overly kindhearted to the person who shot and killed his next of kin.

Tex grabs his saddlebags, rifle and bedroll and jumps out the window onto the Hotel's corrugated iron-roof. Quite a large crowd has gathered in the street down below, and when Tex is sighted, loud calls of warnings echo to warn the Sheriff and Deputies of Tex's escape. Tex sprints along the uneven roof towards the Livery stable, not worrying about the other four members of the gang.

It's each one for himself now, and they sure as hell won't die without him. If they get caught, it'll be their problem, but no Lawman's going to have it out with him, not today or any other day for that matter. Tex doesn't have any dreams of rotting in jail, nor for hanging at the end of a rope. Without thinking twice, Tex jumps the ten feet or so from the roof to the ground when he reaches the Livery.

Landing solidly on his feet, he suddenly groans and goes down on one knee, grabbing his left ankle. He sprained it when landing on the ground, but he can't let something that small keep him from freedom. Getting up, he hobbles into the stables, looking for his horse. He sees his Pinto straight away, and grabbing a saddle, hastily saddles it. With practiced expertize, Tex jumps into the saddle, breaking ground with lightning speed.

Josh, Slick, and the remaining two outlaws hear the three shots, and then the commotion outside. They are unaware of exactly what has happened until they see Tex on the Hotel roof, running like a bat out of hell. It's only when they become aware that the Sheriff and his Deputies are trying to capture Tex, that they decide he needs their help, and forget all else. Without any further ado, the four men walk calmly towards the stables.

Once inside, they take the closest saddles available to them and, saddling their own horses, ride out like they're going for a casual ride. However, one of the Deputies sees them, realizing that they aren't from around these parts, and sounds the alarm. In an instant there are about a dozen or so men after them on horseback, the Sheriff and his two Deputies taking the lead.

Josh turns around in his saddle, as does Slick, firing off shots at the pursuing party. Immediately two Deputies are flung from horseback, causing dust-clouds to rise where they fall. They do not get up again. Slick fires four more shots, making three of them count.

The last one is the Sheriffs. A bullet from Josh's gun hits him in the right eye, and disintegrates the back of his skull. Suddenly the chase is over, and they can focus their attention on catching up with Tex.

Tex is aware that four horses are following him, and gaining ground on him rapidly. He allows his Pinto to slow down a little, so as not to burn him out too early in the chase.

Squinting his eyes against the glare of the sun, he recognizes the horses after a second look. And sure as Candy Cotton sticks, it's the remaining four of his gang! Tex holds up, and waits for them to reach him, but nevertheless, ready for any conflict of interest.

"Whoa! Hey Tex, where you off to in such a bloody hurry, an' where's Justin? You guys have a fallin' out or somethin'?", Josh enquires.

"Yeah, you might say so. We had a difference of opinion, and well, he got the short end of the stick. Stopped three bullets by the way, and he's now as cold as a mornin' winter-breeze. Anyone object to that? Josh, you wanna say somethin'?

"Naw, I ain't got no complaints, Tex. Was plannin' on doin' somethin' 'bout him myself once the chance presented itself. Just never did, an' you beat me to it. Simple as that, man."

"Okay, well, if everything's still alright with you fella's, we're gonna go on West, but I wanna send a scout to check out the next town we're headed for. Just in case there's a surprise waitin' for us at the other end.

Slick, I want to send you ahead. You know these here parts better'n we do. Be careful, an' don't get into a fight about anything with the locals, cos they tend to stand together when there's trouble facing their town. Los Alamos lies about three day's fast riding from here. If you're not back in five days from today, I'll know that you've run into some trouble. We will then carry on to the next town. Enjoy your stay, and don't shoot off at the mouth."

"I'm as solid as a rock when it comes to keeping a secret. Thought you'd have known that by now. People who shoot off at the mouth, more often than not end up in a pine coffin, and I don't intend shortening my life right at this point in time. Don't worry, I'll be on the look-out for anything strange that doesn't fit the picture, but I'm sure there won't be anythin' crawlin' outta the woodwork."

Slick gives a smile that will make the Madonna oil-painting smile back at him, showing off his perfect white teeth. They look like soldiers standing to attention.

"Yeah, yeah, whatever the hell you say. Just don't prove yourself wrong, an' listen to what I'm tellin' you. Stay the hell away from any trouble, or else you're on your own. Did that piece of advice sink into your thick skull? I doubt it, but never mind, just see that you do as you're told."

Tex wants to wipe the grin off Slick's face, but switches his mind to more important things. There isn't any time now for petty behavior, since their lives are at stake here, and it's up to him to find a way out of this mess, seeing as he is the one who landed them all in it. "Well, Tex thinks, as long as they obey his orders, they'll be just fine."

Josh, Pete and John manage to get hold of some cash by selling a few valuables that they acquired along the way; more like taking or stealing than anything else. Each of them hand Slick five dollars, so he can at least buy himself something to eat and drink when he reaches the next town.

Slick thanks them and sets off in a Northerly direction, hoping to make the next small town before nightfall. He knows, like all the rest, that there is no way the next towns down the line will be able to get news of what happened back in Fort Sumner.

Tex and the others watch as Slick quickly disappears over the horizon, and hopes that he will be lucky enough to find Los Alamos open and friendly to invite them in.

CHAPTER SEVEN

Jake has been hanging around Los Alamos now for two days. He is given free boarding and lodging by Sheriff Luke Johnson, who will not hear of Jake staying at the hotel. He has his wife prepare the spare bedroom for the duration of his stay. Sheriff Luke Johnson offers his help, but because his wife is carrying their first-born, Jake refuses to take him up on the offer, although he knows that he will most pro- bably need some backup.

Four days later nobody thinks anything of it when a haggard stranger enters town on horseback. He just barely clings to life with his last bit of fighting spirit. It's an awful day. The wind is blowing up a storm of sand that fills every crevice and shapes new sand dunes.

It isn't a day to spend any time outside, let alone ride on horseback. Jake has become fidgety and edgy. He has been travelling for so long now, that he can't stay in-house for too long before becoming bored. Ronnie has been in his thoughts a lot during these past few days, giving him time to think and brood over his future with her.

The stranger can barely sit upright in his saddle, and when his horse comes to a halt in front of Doc Newman's house, he all but collapses. The Doc's wife, escorted by two men, hurry outside to catch hold of the man. They reach his horse just in time to catch him as he slides from his saddle.

He is attended to urgently, as his health is in a bad state. Doctor Newman's wife puts the patient to bed after he is treated.

She is a qualified sister, and checks in on the man every four hours to see whether any improvement has occurred in the meantime. Doc sends for Jake and Sheriff Luke Johnson, as he was told to do should any stranger come by for treat-

ment of any kind.

Jake is filled with excitement and anticipation as he walks with Luke to find out who this stranger is who has abruptly and out of nowhere shown up in their midst, half dead. Doc Newman awaits their arrival, and promptly tells them that his patient is suffering from malnutrition and exhaustion, as well as dehydration. They want to speak to the man, whose identity is still unknown to them.

The Doc cannot help them here, as he doesn't have any identification on him. They will have to wait three to four days before being able to speak to him and become any the wiser. Doc refuses to let him have any visitors before he's strong enough, whether it's the Law or not. He makes it clear that he will not tolerate any funny business with any patient of his. Jake and Luke have to abide by those rules, whether they like it or not.

Three grueling days later, Doctor Newman sends a young boy over to call them as promised. The stranger is much better, and feels up to having a little talk, although he has not been told who his visitors are going to be. Entering the room where Doc's patient lies, Jake feels the blood rush through his veins when he comes face to face with the man.

Pete Harris, another of Tex's hangers-on, looks at the door expectantly when it opens and two men step inside. Both men are equally surprised to see one another, but this quickly changes. Pete's expression of surprise changes to one of utter horror. He cringes up in bed, backing away, yet there's nowhere to go; he is walled in.

Jake's surprise grows to such a level of hatred when he thinks back to that horrific night, that it seems his chest is going to burst with the size of it. His first instinct is to shoot and kill this varmint he is now facing. Despite all his control, he finds his hand on his gun-butt, burning to draw.

Jake feels a hand on his arm, restricting it from any further movement. Luke lets go of Jake's arm when he sees the look in his eyes. He has never seen an iceberg colder than that look in his life before, and it gives him the creeps right down to his little toe.

"Never thought we'd meet up again, did you? And then it's so far from home, ain't it Pete? Your ma and pa are grievin' their hearts out about what you did, an' the path you chose to go. I hope you remember why it is I'm chasin' you fella's. You know what's comin' your way, don't you? I aim to collect my dues. Let's get one thing straight right now. I don't give a damn how long you stay in this here bed. You ain't leavin' town alive. In fact, you ain't leavin' town at all!"

Jake and Luke walk closer as Jake talks, and they're now standing at the foot of the bed, looking down at Pete. He averts Jake's eyes, because he's looking at death; his own. How many times has he not thought of this day, and longed for the opportunity to turn back time.

If he can turn the clock back only a couple of months, he will never do what he had done. Pete's throat is dry and swollen with fear. It feels worse than riding through the desert. He tries to speak, but nothing will come out of his throat, except incoherent, hoarse blubbering. He is sweating with anxiety, and can feel a trickle of sweat run down his back.

"I..., I, Jake; please forgive me for what I done! Never meant to hurt your missus, I swear! Tex instigated the whole shebang, fire an' all, we was just followin' orders. That's the God's honest truth!"

Jake looks at the man lying in bed, noticeably horrified by the sight of him, in fear for his life, and almost feels pity for the situation he's landed himself in.

"Is that all you have to say for yourself, after the hideous crime you committed? Then you have the audacity to try and pin everything that happened on Tex? He isn't innocent; I know he's the brain behind the whole plan. As far as I know nobody held a gun to your head to convince you to do what you did; right? You lowdown, skunk-eatin' Coyote. When you do get up out of this bed, I'll be outside waitin' for you, you can stake your life on that. You took what was mine, belittled her, scathed her, and left her to die in agony. You'll die for that!"

Pete is sobbing by now, wringing his hands together and covering his face, so as not to see the naked hate that lies shallow in the ex-Law man's eyes.

If death comes by any other means, it will be merciful. To die by the hand of a man whose life you have ruined, and to have to look him in the eye, that is torture to the soul.

Sheriff Luke Johnson knows he has no place in this entire matter, he cannot help this man who is lying in front of him in any way. That's the way things are in these parts. Justice prevails only to the ones who seek it by the way of the Law, and the law around here is a sixgun. Jake is justified by avenging the death of his wife. It wasn't by natural causes, and any man will do the same, given the circumstances.

Luke Johnson informs Doctor Newman that he will place two Deputies on duty to watch over the patient, as he is a wanted outlaw on the run. Sheriff Luke Johnson watches the expression on Jake's face, sees the muscles around his jaw-line tighten as Pete is mentioned. He thinks he can feel the desperate urge for justice that fills Jake's whole existence. Luke's wife, Lucy, told him how broken her heart was after she heard his terrible story from Luke. She can, being pregnant herself, imagine the pain he must be going through.

"Women are better equipped and much more sensitive about such things than men are," she says, explaining how she can say that she understands Jake's feelings.

THE GREY OF DAWN FILTERS through the murky shadows of night when the four men ride into the sleepy little town, if it can be called that. There are but a couple of dilapidated buildings, which have seen better days, and are in dire need of some paint and renovation.

They ride throughout the night, basking in the luminescent light of full moon, and do so at a leisurely pace, only stopping now and then at a waterhole to let their horses drink.

Beef jerky is their only solid food on which to survive until they can reach the next town. Now, looking at the still sleeping town in front of them, Tex doubts that their luck has even so much as changed from what it was previously.

It wouldn't have mattered had they missed this place completely, and not stumbled upon it by chance. If it had not been for someone who had lit a match, they would have gone straight by without even knowing that it existed.

"C'mon men, you call this here a town?" Tex asks. "Look at it, even the Rooster that's supposed to crow, is still asleep. I'll bet you that the youngest citizen here has to be older than my Granny! The Hotel looks like it's goin' to fall over, and I'll stake my life that it has no more'n two rooms, an' they ain't big enough to turn sideways in."

Tex looks in amazement at his fellow outlaws, who shrug their shoulders with disinterest, their only thought being the mindblowing probability of a hot meal, a bath, and a bed; in that precise order. Anything else at this stage takes second place, even Tex's protests. This is one time they aren't going to be intimidated by what Tex wants, or thinks.

"Tex, we don't give a damn about who's awake, an' who ain't. That's of no concern to us right now. We want some grub to fill our bellies, we ain't had a decent bath in weeks, an' we're dead beat. Now, you can do whatever it is that you wanna do, but I aim to get exactly what I just spoke about. I'll worry 'bout everythin' else later on."

Josh has spoken his piece, and it may have been a big bite to take, but it's out and in the open, no turning back now. Had it been a couple of days earlier, such behavior would have had dire consequences, but

Tex himself is haggard and also hungry. He doesn't much see the point of making a fuss about Josh's comment.

In fact, he's sure everybody else feels the same way Josh does, they're just too scared to admit or comment to it. He is actually quite sure that if he was to try and make something out of this, the guys will sure as hell back Josh up. Tex look at the men, realizing that out of a gang of eleven able-bodied men, they are now only four.

He feels a pang of disappointment, not towards the men he rides with, but because of the way fate seems to have turned against them. Their short-lived spell of good luck has become an omen, its dark fingers clutching and pulling at their livelihood and existence.

During the past week or so, there has been plenty a moment when his thoughts returned to one evening in Black Rock, and the ghastly crime and sin he and his buddies committed that night. It's haunting him lately, making him lose a lot of sleep, and then there are the nightmares he awakes from when at last he does manage to fall asleep.

Tex has even thought of waiting for that Sheriff, what's his name again? Oh yeah; Jake Hudson, and when he catches up with Tex, hand himself over. Although it seems like the only honorable way to go, Tex doesn't fool himself for one moment. He knows what he would have done if the shoe were on the other foot. As he comes to realize this fact, he finds that he no longer hates the Lawman who is chasing after him.

He feels empathy, and a deep sorrow overwhelms Tex, for he realizes then that he has taken a man's most prized possession from him. Tex knows that he has shattered another human being's life into tiny bits and pieces that can never again be puzzled back together. He too, will have wanted and taken revenge upon the perpetrator of such a deed. His thoughts are interrupted by a storm of words raining down on him.

"Hey, Tex, you comin' or stayin'? We're goin' to look for some grub, even though it's still mighty early. Might just find someone willin' to help us out of our predicament; yes sirree. Hell, I'd give my left wisdom tooth for a piece o' steak, some eggs an' bacon, washed down with steamin' hot coffee!"

Pete smacks his lips loudly.

"What you talkin' 'bout wisdom teeth?

We was under the impression you didn't have no brains to think with. You ain't got no wisdom, Pete, coz that comes with experience."

The other three gang members are pulling Pete's leg, and enjoying every second of it. Pete is happy enough to let it slide, as he knows that he is just being pestered for the sheer fun of it.

"Besides," he thinks, "we could all do with a little laughter. I ain't laughed in months, an' come to think of it, it's quite damn depressin'."

The bantering lifts their spirit a little, making them feel a little more human.

The quiet little town slowly awakens from its peaceful sleep. There is no rush, for it's mostly elderly folk living here. A couple of youngsters are just biding their time before leaving this Godforsaken place to start a life of their own. The town council has been absconded years ago, and there hasn't been a Lawman in this part of the County for fifteen years.

There's no money to pay for upholding the Law. The town's people don't need a Lawman to uphold the Law, because there is no crime in these parts whatsoever, or at least; that's how it has been all these years. All this is about to change drastically within the next couple of hours, unbeknownst to the citizens.

As the small, but neat diner opens its doors at exactly seven thirty, the four newcomers to town tie their horses, and step up onto the boardwalk to enter the diner. People walk about and stare at these strange men, wondering why they're wearing guns. Tex is aware that there is serious discussion because of their appearance.

They're dirty and unshaven, and the color of their clothing is no longer discernible. Tough, unruly men have never been a part of this community, and these folks don't know how to handle men of such caliber. A few youngsters, boys and girls, give the outlaws looks of amazed interest.

Everybody sees and knows that this crowd of men is not to be confronted or crossed in any way. The young woman in the crowd draw special attention from Tex's men, who haven't had a woman in close to six weeks, but filling their bellies now is their top priority.

An exceptionally old woman of small and slender build takes their order. She moves at a snail's pace, most probably protecting frail bones or arthritis. The four outlaws are very much dissatisfied. They shout obscenities at her.

"Hurry up, you old cow. We ain't got all day to wait for our food! Lift them feet and take a run, you old mackerel, and while you're at it, bring us a bottle o' Whisky. Not the cheap stuff you old hag!"

These comments are followed by raucous laughter, and the slapping of hands on table-tops. Upon their entry into town, and it being so early, they have ample time to look around. At first observation they notice that there's no Law office. This means there is no Sheriff around.

This is any outlaw's dream, and in an instant all Tex's good thoughts and sorrowful deeds go down the drain. He isn't going to repent anything concerning the past, turn the other cheek and take a blow. Now is their one and only chance to take their dues. It's going to be like taking candy from a kid, no trouble at all.

They eat like pigs, gulping up the food and swallowing simultaneously. It's obvious that they lack any manners, and the few townsfolk who do enter the small diner, find it revolting. They turn around and leave again. Their food finished, John throws his plate across the floor, shattering it against the counter.

"Your food sucks, old lady! You always cook like this? I'm sure I can find a ten-year old that'll do a better job than this. Bring me some bacon an' eggs, an' make it snappy. You'd better not mess up this time, coz you'll be sorry if you do. Hear me?"

Tex and the rest of the gang start laughing, when a voice interrupts their fun. It comes like a whiplash, making even them jump with surprise.

"Hey mister, who the hell do you think you are to speak to your elders like that! That little lady you've just humiliated for the second time, is my mother. Now, you'll get up off your fat ass, and real dignified, apologize to her, an' you better mean it. If you decide not to abide by my request, I'll kill you where you stand. Men have died for less than that. Are we on the same level here or you want me to draw you a picture?"

There is a stunned silence for a couple of seconds, the outlaws trying to figure out what, and who, has just happened.

"Over here, you shit faced low-lives; behind you! I'm the Chef here, and I do the cooking. You don't like it, go eat someplace else, after you've paid for the food of course, and includin' the pardon to my mother."

John turns red in the face, half rising in his chair. His fellow outlaws smirk at him, and he doesn't like the humiliation one bit. It makes him look like a complete idiot. He'll show this big talker who he is dealing with. Obviously, he isn't aware of the danger

he's in. John turns to face the voice.

"Now look here, mister Chef, you do whatever it is you think you have to, but I ain't gonna sit here and listen to you insultin' me in front o' my friends. An' to tell you the truth, your food tastes like shit. You can't cook to save your life. Your mother, by the looks of it, should've been dead an' buried a long time ago. What you gonna do now, big boy? Go runnin' to your momma, an' clutch at her dress? In case you haven't noticed, there're four of us, an' only one o' you. When we're done with you, you're gonna wish you'd never crossed paths with us, never mind opened up your big trap!"

Tex intervenes.

"John, you caused the trouble, so you sort it out by yourself. We ain't gonna help you. Besides, I think you can take him, he ain't even packin' a gun. If you wanna end this quickly, I'll lend you my gun. Shoot him, so we can take what we want an' quit this one-horse town."

The Chef is immovable.

"You ain't going nowhere in a hurry. Me and you", he says, pointing a finger at John, "we're going outside. There hasn't been a showdown in our town for over twenty years, so I reckon you'll have your couple of minutes of fame before you go down. You're a loser and a no-good low-life skunk."

He turns his gaze to Tex.

"And for your information, I'm packin'."

The man pulls away the left side of his jacket, exposing an Army Colt issue .45 single action, also known as The Peacemaker, stuck into his waistband. It's a heavy weapon with a long barrel for greater accuracy over long distances.

Without any further ado, the Chef turns and walks outside, where a crowd has already started gathering on the boardwalks. One of the youngsters, who overhears the heated argument in the diner, spreads the word faster than a wildfire. Tex gives John his six-gun and holster, and then him and the other three join the rest of the crowd.

There is a buzz of excitement running through the crowd of onlookers, especially from the younger ones, as they have never before witnessed anything like this. Everybody knows that the Chef is a crack shot who can draw his gun with lightning speed without any effort.

John walks some twenty paces before turning around to face his challenger. The man stands erect and quiet, his feet only a little apart, arms dangling loosely at his sides. His Colt .45 isn't holstered, but nonchalantly sticks from his waistband at an angle. John sees this, and thinks that it looks mighty unhandy to draw in this manner, which will also make the man slower than usual.

He'll be an easy target, and a sitting

duck, as John surmises that he will outdraw this man in a flash, killing him before he even knows what has hit him. John allows himself a lopsided grin, thinking how afraid these people will be after he's killed the 'town hero'.

They'll do as and when he requests anything. With these thoughts churning in his mind, John focuses on the man facing him, feeling a little intimidated by his cool attitude.

The man's eyes stare fixedly at John's face, not blinking at all. He is looking for that flicker of an eyelid, or the twitching of a face-muscle. In most cases, it gives away the fact that the opponent is about to make his move. John's eyes start burning, for he can't keep his eyes open without blinking.

"To hell with it," John thinks, "I'm gonna smoke him and get it over with. The hell with him an' his old lady. They can kiss my ass!"

John's mouth twitches, and his right hand snakes downwards, his curled fingers closing around the gun butt. His thumb is already pulling back the hammer. In a split second, John clears the gun from its sheath, bringing his hand up to squeeze the trigger. He never sees the man opposite him move, just feels the hot lead as it burns a hole in his gut.

John reels back, grasping his belly, at the same time seeing the blood; his blood, spill through his fingers. Then he hears the loud bang. As he tries to raise his hand to fire a shot, the second and third bullets smack into the left side of his face and chest, sending him somersaulting backwards with the impact. John dies before he hits the ground, never having the opportunity to think of anything else except the pain that registers in his brain before death takes him.

There is a loud cheering from the crowd of onlookers. The man, whom the outlaws have come to name ole Greasy, walks over to where John lies, bends over and takes the six-gun from his lifeless fingers. He turns to face Tex.

"I'll be taking this here gun, mister. Don't seem to me to be doing any of you any good. In fact, I think it'll keep you outta trouble long enough to stay alive while you're here. I aim to help you even more by giving you and your men ten minutes to get out of our town. We don't take kindly to your particular breed, seeing as we're a loving community, peaceful and kind, and we don't stand for outsiders to disturb the balance we've created."

Tex, Josh and Pete are ushered and escorted not so politely, out of town, and helped on their way. After a couple of miles, Pete calls his horse to a halt. Tex and Josh also stop, thinking that Pete wants to take a rest, but the latter is rattled and shaken.

"Tex, Josh, I'm goin' my own way from here on in. There're three of us left. Eight of our gang have been taken out in two months. That's alarming man. I think if each of us goes our own way, the chances of catching up with us are much smaller than if we stick together. I wanna start afresh, turn over a new leaf where nobody knows anythin' about me, or what I done up to now. I'm still headin' North, so I guess I won't be seein' you around pretty soon, huh? Stay well, an' thanks for everything Tex. You too, Josh. We seen us a helluva lot o' good times, didn't we, but these last couple o' months together wasn't much fun. We've lost more than we gained. Well, best of luck to you two. Yeee-hah!"

Pete turns his horse facing North-ward, and puts the spurs to him, waving as he speeds away.

Tex looks at Josh, shrugging his shoulders as he does so.

"Well Josh, I guess what Pete's said, has a ring of truth to it. I'm headin' due West, reckon Phoenix in Arizona'll do it. It's a nice big city, and one could easily get lost there. You ridin' with me, or you also plan on goin' your own way?"

Josh shakes his head.

"Naw, reckon I'll be ridin' with you, Tex. I ain't plannin' on settling down right now. Phoenix sounds good to me. I never been there myself, but Justin's told me quite a bit about it. Sounds excitin', and the women are, accordin' to Justin's say-so, extremely beautiful and willin'. So off we go."

With a swirl of their Stetsons, and a wild cry that echoes away into the distance, they put their horses to a fast gallop in a Westerly direction.

PETE HAS NOW BEEN TRAVELLING for almost three days, and each river he's come across during this time, has been dry to the bed. The last water he comes across, is at the Pecos River, miles and miles behind him. His canteen quickly runs dry after he leaves the Pecos river.

He doesn't have a lot to eat, either. Fortunately, his horse has plenty of grass to feed on, and this is at least a little moist. As for Pete, he can feel that so little water and scarcity of food is starting to take its toll on him. Soon they will be out of the grasslands and in open, rocky country, where there's no water at all. What scares him most of all, is that he doesn't know for sure how far the next town is.

It can be days, or even weeks, before he reaches civilization. His lips are parched and dry, the skin peeling off at places, and he's been sweating profusely. Pete is no Doctor, but even he knows that if he keeps on sweating like this without taking in water, he will dehydrate very quickly.

Night comes suddenly and without war-

ning, covering everything in its mystical darkness. Pete has been too pre-occupied with his thoughts to notice that dusk, and then darkness is busy setting in.

Looking around and squinting his eyes in the dark, Pete finds there is enough moonlight to find small sticks and branches to build a fire. He rolls some grass into a loose ball, and places it on top of the thickest stick that he manages to find. Quickly he rubs another stick vertically and with force, until the bottom stick starts smoking, then puts the grass ball on top of it and blows softly. The branch begins to smolder, and then, instantly, it's alight.

Quickly Pete stacks more wood on top, making as large a fire as he can with the branches and other sticks he's managed to find in the surrounding area.

"One helluva fire, an' nothin' to cook on it. Don't help me much, bein' as hungry as I am. A couple more days, an I'll be ready to eat my horse if it comes down to it."

Pete shudders at this thought, for he knows he will never be able to eat the flesh of the horse that he's been riding on. That will just be a ghastly and beastly thing to do. No, he'll be in a town within the next day or two, he's sure of that.

Then he'll ask for a plate of food, instead of doing something that will get him into trouble. That will be his first step to becoming a better person, and starting a new life. Pete curls up in his bedroll close to the fire, and ignoring the hunger pains, thinks of his new life he is going to lead. With this vision uppermost in his thoughts, he at last falls asleep, tiredness replacing hunger.

CHAPTER EIGHT

It's been ten days since Pete's arrival in Los Alamos, clinging to life with near super-human strength, escaping death by perhaps a few hours. Had it not been for the exquisite and professional care of Doc Newman and his wife, Pete knows that he would have been dead meat. That would have been a much more graceful way to die than what he faces at this moment.

He is fully recovered by now, has been for almost five days. Pete is trying to buy himself some time to devise a plan to get out of this one alive. No matter how he plans it, he just can't see his way out. Firstly, there's the Deputy who looks in on him every thirty minutes, not to mention the one outside who is stationed right in front of the bedroom window.

He only leaves his post when another Deputy relieves him. His chances of getting away undetected are less than zero. Pete also knows that any day now Jake Hudson will be coming for him, knowing that he is playing for time.

There's a knock on his door, and the door handle turns. Missus Newman, whom he has come to like because of her soft and caring nature, comes inside with freshly baked bread just out of the oven, and a large glass of cold milk. Fresh butter is spread thick on the bread, and on the side is a knife to spread some jam if he chooses to.

"Thank you, missus Newman. This bread's delicious, as always, plus your food is making me gain weight. I wouldn't be surprised if my clothes don't fit me no longer. I really am a lucky fella to have such a good person like yourself look after me. "

"Now, now, you don't want an old lady like me blushing, do you? Flattery will get you everywhere, young fellow. But for now, you'll have to be content with a few slices of bread. I'll bring you something nice to eat a little later on, some home-made cookies and strong coffee, just the way you like it. Sound good?"

"Yeah, sounds great; I can't wait. Heard the Doc talking just now. Any new patients come in today?"

"No my boy; no sick people today. It was that Sheriff, uhm, what's his name again? It's that nice, tall man who came to pay you a visit the other day. Oh yes, now I remember, Hudson is his surname. He was just enquiring about your state of health, said you had to be recovered by now, and that he would be here tomorrow morning to take you with him. Oh, it's such a pity, this thing he has hanging over your head. You're still so young, and I've grown so fond of you, even though you did make some harsh mistakes."

At the door, she turns and looks at Pete with an expression of sorrow etched into her soft features. He thinks he sees tears in her eyes. Does she perhaps wish that she can help him? If so, what is she prepared to do? She closes the door, and he can hear her footsteps carry down the corridor towards the front of their home.

Pete has a sick feeling on the pit of his stomach when he thinks about the following day and Jake Hudson. Even Tex, when he speaks about the Lawman, does so with fear and respect. Tex had once warned all of them.

"That Sheriff from Black Rock ain't nobody's fool. We chose the wrong person to cross paths with, and wrong him in the worst possible way. He's coming with a vengeance far greater than anybody could possibly hate another human being. I heard when he told someone I know, who lives in Black Rock, that vengeance is a dish best served cold. That gives me the creep's, man. Know what I mean?"

Pete now knows what Tex had meant that day, but doesn't pay much attention to what he says. He knows that he only has today still to make his move, and it will have to be one that will outsmart everybody. He'll have to have the edge.

Then it comes to him in a flash. Why didn't he think of it earlier? Yes, that's it, there's no other way out of this mess, and even though he detests what he is about to do, he knows that she will understand.

With this in mind, he will just have to put the Deputy outside his door out of action first, before he can make even one move. This is crucial in his plan. What makes it so good is that nobody is going to expect him to do such a thing. Pete almost laughs aloud when he thinks of everything coming together so suddenly.

He no longer has any regrets about his past, he can only think of getting away from under the watchful and vengeful eye of that Sheriff. Yeah, he will disappear and start a new life somewhere else, in a small town where nobody will ask any unnecessary questions.

Pete lies back against his pillow after finishing the bread and milk, feeling satisfied with himself. The knife that he uses to spread the jam on his bread, has been tucked away out of sight under his pillow. Missus Newman won't miss the knife when she comes by later to fetch his plate. He's going to sleep for a couple of hours to be alert and fresh.

He turns on his side, facing the door, and within a couple of minute's he is sound asleep. Finding that all is peaceful and in order, the Deputy smiles and closes the door, thinking that he can very easily get used to a cozy job like this. Why, missus Newman bakes the best bread in the County, and her cookies are delicious with coffee. Yeah, life is good ...

XXX

The large Grandfather clock in the foyer of Doc Newman's home chimes six times, announcing that it's exactly six o'clock. Dinner is served at six thirty, and Pete is actually looking forward to having dinner, as he has not eaten much of the cookies brought to him a little earlier the afternoon. Missus Newman hasn't noticed that the knife is not on the plate, or if she had, she didn't say anything about it.

The afternoon nap had done him well; he feels as sharp as a razor, and has his get-away planned to the smallest detail. The guards change shifts at ten o'clock. He will jump the relieving guard after he has had time to get the other part of his plan to work.

As these thoughts race through his criminal mind, the door opens, and missus Newman enters with his dinner. It smells good, and although his mind is pre-occupied with other things, he makes friendly conversation with missus Newman for a while. During this time, he asks whether he will be allowed to make himself a cup of coffee at around ten thirty before retiring to bed. Missus Newman chuckles softly.

"My dear boy, I wouldn't let you make

coffee for yourself. You're our guest, and a sick one on top of it. We're still awake by that time, so I'll personally bring you some coffee, and if you're good, I might slip some cookies in too. Now, doesn't that sound a lot better than getting up so late and making your own? You men can't look after yourselves anyway."

"You're too kind. I'm going to miss you a lot, not to mention your cooking and the treats."

Things couldn't have been going better for him, he thinks as missus Newman excuses herself and leaves the room to tend to her husband's needs.

At 9:45PM, Pete gets out of his bed,

and without making the slightest noise, opens the cupboard where his clothes have been hanging now for the past ten days. Missus Newman washed and ironed them, and a quick look puts him at ease. Even his boots are polished, and she has given him a new pair of socks that she especially went out to buy for him at the shop.

He goes to the nightstand, and bending over it, he washes his face and rubs his hair with his wet hands. Just then, he hears voices outside in the corridor, and without warning, the door opens as the new Deputy sticks his head around it.

"Hi there, I'll be around till tomorrow morning. You want anything, give me a shout, but I'm hoping we'll have a peaceful night's rest. Just behave your-

self, and we won't have any trouble."

The Deputy doesn't ask why Pete is out of bed, nor does he seem to care for the reason. He knows that Pete can't go out the window, so it's safe. He pulls back, closing the door behind him.

Outside, the other Deputy waits impatiently for his relief, muttering under his breath as he strides up and down. Finally, it's time, and Pete watches as the two Deputies exchange greetings, accompanied by a little chit-chat. Then the one Deputy says goodbye and departs.

"Good, now both Deputies have been relieved, and within the next fifteen minutes I'll be getting my coffee", Pete thinks. "I'm almost free, just another couple minutes. Thanks, missus Newman; you'll never realize just how much you really helped me!"

A knock on his door brings him back to reality.

"Come in, the door ain't locked. Oh, time for my coffee already, is it?"

Just then the Deputy pops his head around the door, looking around the room.

"You okay, ma'am? Harrison, you still behaving yourself in the presence of this here lady? Give me a shout if he tries anything, missus Newman, and I'll stick his head where the sun don't shine."

Missus Newman looks from Pete to the

Deputy, responding with her usual friendliness.

"Why don't you come in and have some coffee, young man? There's enough to go around, so why waste any?"

"Well ma' am, you see, I ain't exactly supposed to interact on a personal level with the prisoner here. The Sheriff will rip my heart out if he found out that I was socializing instead of doing my job. You know how strict he is when it comes to us doing our job like he says it's gotta be done. You also know he don't accept no excuses for foul-ups. I think I'd rather stay out here, if you don't mind."

The Deputy, without noticing, steps

inside Pete's room about five feet, and doesn't pay any attention to Pete who stands at the dressing table when he enters. Missus Newman unknowingly lures the Deputy into Pete's trap by inviting him in for coffee, thus taking his attention off Pete.

Pete sees his chance and takes it. The Deputy stands with his back half-turned towards Pete. He's about to retreat, when Pete lunges forward, at the same time pulling the hidden knife from his waistband. Before the Deputy knows what's happening, Pete presses the blade against his throat with so much force, that he draws a thin line of blood. At the same time he snatches the Deputies gun from its holster and steps back, out of reach of the Deputy. Without taking his eyes off him, he addresses the Doctors wife.

"Now, missus Newman, you tie the Deputy up, an' stuff a sock or something in his mouth, so he don't get a notion to shout for help. You hear me good, Lawman, one whisper outta you, and you're history. I'll shoot you where you stand, got me? You let me leave without a ruckus an' I'll let you live to grow old, else your kids are goin' to grow up without their daddy. The choice is yours. An' you old lady, come on over here. I think I'll take you with me for company, for a while at least, till I'm sure nobody else is followin' us. Then I'll let you go."

The shocked expression in Irene Newman's eyes makes Pete look away. He feels a tug of disappointment in himself, but it's too late now to make things undone. He has to finish what he's started, if he wants to survive past this night.

"C'mon, we ain't got all night. Where's the Doc, he still awake?"

Irene Newman looks at Pete, disgust alive in her eyes, her face expressionless and cold as stone.

"Yes, but he's waiting in bed for me. Please don't hurt him, he wouldn't swat a fly."

"Don't worry none about the Doc, I ain't gonna hurt him. He helped me recover from my ordeal, as did you. Sorry; but there's no other means of escape for me, except doin' it this way. I want you to know that I mean you no harm, coz all you've done is be good to me, but I gotta have some leverage. That Sheriff from Black Rock wants to see me hanged, an' I ain't prepared or willin' to die now or in the close future."

Pete gags and ties the Deputy up and stuffs him in the cupboard, locking it. He pushes Irene Newman out in front of him and into the hallway, closing the door behind him.

"Lead the way ma'am, an' don't scream or start runnin', coz then I will shoot you. Understand that?"

"Irene, you coming to bed?"

It's Doc Newman enquiring from out of their bedroom.

He hears voices in the hallway, and assumes that it's his wife talking to the night-shift deputy. His wife told him that she was going to take Pete a last cup of coffee before retiring to bed, but he is now starting to grow a little impatient.

"Irene, what's keeping you? It's getting late. Leave them youngsters be, they can look after themselves. Besides, there're two Deputies on duty to keep watch. Come on to bed now, will you?"

The house is dead quiet, and he can't hear Irene's voice either anymore. Frowning, he gets up out of bed and walks to the bedroom doorway, looking in the direction of Pete's room. He expects to see his wife walking towards their room, but only a dark emptiness greets him.

Then the Doc hears the front door open and close. Alarmed, he walks down the corridor towards Pete's room, and when he hears nothing after he knocks, he turns the doorknob and enters. He looks to where he expects to find Pete lying on his bed, but he stares at an empty bed.

"What in blazes is going on, and where is Irene and this young fellow?", Doc Newman mumbles aloud.

Suddenly Doc Newman realizes that he has not seen the Deputy in the corridor either.

"Where is everybody tonight?"

There's a faint noise coming from the cupboard, and reluctantly Doc walks towards it, not knowing what to expect. He slowly opens the cupboard door, standing half behind it. The Deputy, who falls against the inside of the door, loses his balance and lands on the ground in front of Doc Newman's feet, staring up at him with widespread eyes.

He thinks that it's Pete who has decided to return and finish him off. There is a moment of stunned silence in the room, then the Deputy signals to Doc Newman to untie him and take the gag out of his mouth. Quickly the Deputy tells Doc what has happened, asking him for one of his guns. The Sheriff and Jake Hudson have to be informed of the latest development. Pete already has a head start of about twenty minutes on them.

Luckily, Luke Johnson and Jake are not in bed yet when the Deputy arrives in a frantic state of mind, with Doc Newman and the second Deputy in tow. After hearing what has happened, both men saddle their horses in record time. Sheriff Luke Johnson asks his wife to take care of the shocked Doc Newman, as he is too old to partake in the chase after Pete.

Jake and the other three lawmen leave town at high speed, the full moon their only guide in tracing the tracks. The tracks are still very fresh, undisturbed. After riding for about half an hour, they come to an abrupt stop. In front of them, clearly silhouetted against the moonlight, about fifty feet or so, missus Newman's horse is calmly eating grass. She is sitting upright on the horse, her head bowed, as if in prayer. Jake rides up to her.

"You okay, missus Newman?"

She lifts her head and Jake sees that she has been crying.

"Yes, I'm fine, thank you mister Hudson. I just can't believe that Pete did such a thing, and then used me to get away. Doesn't he have a heart? I would never have thought that he could be so conniving and treacherous. At least he wasn't violent towards me, so I suppose I have to thank my lucky stars for that."

Luke Johnson turns to one of his Deputies and says "Take missus Newman

home, and see she gets there unscathed. Hurry it up; Doc must be worried sick by now. As a matter-of-fact, I think you should both turn back. You go tell my wife I'll be back after this has been settled."

Both deputies turn their horses around and leading Irene Newman's horse, take off towards town. Luke waits until the trio has disappeared before he speaks up.

"Ole missus Newman looks okay to me, don't she Jake? I wonder if she had anything to do with that Harris fellow giving us the slip tonight. You think she was inclined to help him? I'm telling you, I have my doubts about the way things played out tonight, but I'll rather keep 'em to myself. No use in waking up sleeping dogs with accusations I can't prove. I'll bet you're thinking the exact same thing as me."

Luke Johnson doesn't wait for an answer from Jake, but instead spurs his horse forward.

"Let's get going. That outlaw's gained a lot of distance on us by now."

"Yeah, I suppose you're right. We've had about a twenty minute rest, so we can push our horses. Jet's eager to put some miles under his hoofs, so let's not waste

any more time."

"Where d'you think he's headed, Jake? You know him better than me. You think he's goin' towards Tex and the other men? If he is, we'd better see that we track him down before he gets to them, wherever that might be."

"Dunno Luke, he might be headin' for Arizona, the way I see it. Probably Phoenix. He's ridin' in a pretty straight Westerly direction, an' he's covering a lot of ground very fast. If he keeps it up, we might be in luck, coz he's goin' to exhaust those horses before long, or lame one o' them."

Jake is shouting to make himself heard above the thunder of pounding hooves, and Luke Johnson gives a thumbs up to indicate that he has heard Jake and agrees with it.

After an hour and a half of hard riding, with two ten-minute intervals of slowing down in between, Jake spots a dark speck far ahead of them. He points at it to make Luke aware of the fast travelling rider ahead of them.

Jake and Luke Johnson have now been travelling for almost four hours, and Jake pulls his horse in. He doesn't think there is any point in both of them chasing after one man.

"Luke, I think it would be best if you returned to Los Alamos. You have a kid on the way, and besides, it would be good if you could send a telegram to all the town's Sheriffs up ahead. Warn them of what's coming their way, just in case. You can also inform 'em of my role in the chase. That'll give me the lea-way of not having to explain to everybody who I am every time I have to stop off somewhere."

"You sure you'll be okay? I could ride with you till day-break; it ain't no sweat off my back."

Jake shakes his head, saying "I'm fine, Luke. I plan on catchin' up with Pete Harris before he reaches his destination. Besides, my horse is used to ridin' hard and long hours, an' I'm also used to bein' in the saddle for hours at a time. Something else, I don't want your blood on my hands; I can't cope with that. Say goodbye to your wife for me, and thank you for all your hospitality. Good luck with the little one!"

The two men shake hands, and Jake speeds away on Jet's back, giving him free reins to run as he chooses. A cool night breeze keeps Jake alert and fresh. He feels confident that he will now start gaining some lost ground on Pete, for Pete's horse has to be getting pretty close to very tired by now. Turning all his attention to the chase that lies ahead, Jake lowers himself in the saddle behind Jet's large head, listening to the animals' rhythmic breathing as he runs.

Dawn breaks, and by the looks of it, it promises to scorch everything that comes across its burning rays. It's still very early, and grey misty clouds hang in the sky like cloaks of light cotton wool. In between the contrast of sharp orange and bright yellow that tries to break through the misty clouds, a soft pastel blue can be seen.

Suddenly the shadows are gone, and the full intensity of the early morning heat makes mirrors on the earth's crust. Jake is sure that he's crossed over into Arizona, because the territory around and in front of him is very rocky. The ground looks dry, but Jake knows that there are numerous rivers running through this State.

He isn't worried about water. Pete is his biggest concern at this stage, for he could be lying behind any large boulder right at this minute, waiting for Jake to come closer so he'll have a better shot at him.

Jake decides to dismount, and moves underneath a colossal overhanging rock-face. He takes out his binoculars, and places them in front of his eyes. Slowly and patiently, Jake scours the country that lies in front and to the right of him. He sees a movement half a mile up from where he is, but can't be sure.

It's too quick. It could be a rabbit or other small rodent. Jake concentrates the binoculars on that specific spot, and waits patiently. Ten minutes drag by; feeling like hours. There it is again, this time more distinguishable. It's the reflection of the sun on ...

The impact of the bullet spins Jake around like a top. He is hit, but it's more of a burn than a wound. He takes the bullet in his left armpit, just as he lifts his arms for a closer look at the spot where he sees the movement.

It hurts like hell, although the bullet hasn't penetrated his flesh. There's also a lot of blood, as there always is with superficial wounds. His skin has just been split open, causing small veins to burst.

Jake quickly takes his kerchief and shoves it inside his shirt underneath his armpit, closing his arm to apply pressure on the small wound. The reflection that he saw, had been the sun reflecting off of a rifle barrel.

"How could I have been so careless and clueless? Should've known he wasn't going to give up so easily. What a dumb ass I've been!", he scolds himself.

Jake feels like knocking himself in the head for being such a walkover. Pete Harris must've been laughing at him while he squeezed the trigger. Jake comes up onto one knee in the meantime, and taking hold of the reins, pulls himself up with one arm.

There is suddenly the sound of hooves on rocky ground, the sound growing closer by the second. Then the horse appears around the outcrop of the rock-face, the rider looking down at Jake, smiling.

The smile on Pete's face quickly makes place for one of shock and bewilderment as he realizes that Jake is not dead, but very much alive, and has sustained only a minor injury. The rifle that Jake was shot with, has been put back into its sheath beside the saddle, and Pete nonchalantly rides up to where Jake is, sure that his shot has killed Jake.

Pete starts stammering, then, when

He realizes that Jake doesn't have a gun in his hand, stops. His hand streaks down to his side, where he holstered the gun that he took from the Deputy the previous night.

"You're dead meat, Lawman! This time I'll make sure you eat the bullet, an' ride it to Hell an' back, you dog! The shoe's on the other foot now, ain't it? I'll be known as the quickest gun who killed the famous Jake Hudson of Black Rock. You feel pretty dumb right now, huh? Well, too bad you ... "

"You talk too much, Harris. If you were as good a shot as you are a preacher, I would've been dead now. Didn't your daddy teach you not to talk so much? Too much talkin' can get you
killed."

Pete doesn't even see Jake's hand move, he only looks down the muzzle of the biggest gun he has ever seen in his life, or so it seems.

He becomes aware of a pain so intense that he can't think. It clouds his judgment, and he can't stop falling.

Jake's first bullet takes Pete high in the chest, throwing him over backwards. The second and third bullets' smack into Pete simultaneously, taking out both his eyes and exiting his head at the base of his skull, obliterating the entire brainstem and instantly killing him.

Jake takes hold of Pete's horse's reins, mounts Jet, and without as much as a second look at Pete's now lifeless body, rides off at a leisurely pace in search of a railway station. He has decided to take the train to Phoenix, instead of riding all the way. The trip will be quicker, and he'll arrive at his destination before Tex and the remaining member of the outlawed gang.

CHAPTER NINE

Jake reaches a railway station in Bisbee belonging to the Western Pacific Railway Company. It's quite a large station, for this is built to accommodate a fast-growing population. More and more people are descending upon the West, for land is cheap and vast in these regions, and cattle farmers are making money like it grows on trees.

There are quite a few people waiting for the train to arrive, ready to board as soon as it stops, for the train keeps a tight schedule and only fills up with water before departing again. Fortunately, there is a cargo truck attached to the back of the train, where everything else, including livestock, is loaded. Jake first makes sure that Jet is aboard before boarding himself, taking a seat at the window.

A little jerk and Jake feels the train move forward, quickly picking up speed and heading for its next stop. After a while the conductor comes around to clip the tickets. He is short and excessively overweight, but very friendly, talking to everybody as he comes down the aisle. It looks like he enjoys his work.

"He gets paid to travel and see the whole of the country, one could say. No wonder he is so happy", Jake thinks to himself.

"Ticket, please sir. Ah, going to Phoenix, I see. Lovely city, and so much to do. The ladies are very pretty up there. We have six more stops to make before we hit Phoenix. I'll give you a call a couple miles before we get there, if you like."

"Thank you", Jake replies. "I'd appreciate that. I wanna get some shut-eye in the meantime; been travelin' some distance on horse-back, and the sittin' down has made me quite tired."

"Don't you worry none, sir. I'll give
you a shout about fifteen minutes or so before we hit Phoenix. Give
you enough time to rest peacefully. Enjoy your ride with us."

One thing is for sure. Tex and whomever is travelling with him,
can't just ride into Tombstone and do what they like. The law there is
much too hard on men with the likes of them, and ordinary folk have
found out that fighting back against criminals help to a degree.

Jake hopes that he won't have to wait in vain for Tex to show up
in Tombstone, because he has an idea that the latter is about to change
all his plans he's made thus far. It will put Jake right back to square
one, exactly where he was five months ago when he started the chase.
The last two or three miles while the train runs effortlessly on the rail
along the mountainside, Jake appreciates the view in all it's splendor
presented to him.

Just then the conductor comes to inform him that they will be
stopping at the station in Tombstone within the next fifteen minutes or
so. Jake thanks him, and gets up from his seat to collect his belongings
from the overhead shelf.

The train's speed decreases, and it rolls into Tombstone at a snail's
pace. Without any further ado, Jake collects his belongings, and when
the train comes to a standstill, he gets off and walks towards the back
of the train cars where Jet has been riding in the cargo truck.

The door to the stable-car is already open and the horses are exiting.
Jet comes down the carriage-walk, wild-eyed and snorting anxiously.
It's his first time to be transported by rail, and by the looks of it, he
doesn't at all agree to the bumpy ride. He is fidgety and his nostrils flare
wide.

"Okay pardner, you can relax now, the ride's over", Jake says as he
strokes Jet's mane. "We're goin' to be waitin' for them outlaws here. I
doubt they'll be expectin' to find us here, that's to say if they plan on
comin' through this way, which I hope they do, to tell you the honest
truth. It'll mean the end of the long haul for us, Jet. Then we can head

back to Texas and start a new life."

Jake enters the Sheriff's office without knocking. Sitting with his feet crossed on the table in front of him, rolling his six-gun's bullet chamber slowly around, is a lanky man. Tall and well built, yet not bulky in size. He looks up as Jake enters the office, at the same time giving him a once-over. Jake offers his hand.

"Howdy. Saw the light burnin', so I decided to come on in an' introduce myself. Name's Jake Hudson."

"Glad to finally meet you, Jake. Born Joseph Evans, but please, call me Joe for short. I'm the U.S Deputy Marshal here in Tombstone. I see you're a bit surprised? Let me explain. Got a telegram here from a Sheriff Luke Johnson down in Los Alamos, explainin' who you are, and what you're doing around these parts. I expected you a little sooner, but I also know what it's like on the trail. These fella's you're after; what do they look like? I'll get the sketch artist to make a look-alike drawing of the suspects, then we can post 'em all over town, and I'll send some of 'em to the next towns with the Stage-coach driver. Been lookin' for a strange face since last week, without any success. Like I said, I was expecting you sooner than today. Let's do some talkin'."

Jake takes a seat in the chair Deputy Marshal Joe Evans waves to. Without beating about the bush, Joe Evans comes right to the point.

"As you yourself know, being an ex-Lawman, the Laws have changed a lot these last couple of years, especially when it comes to shooting people in public. Oh, you and I know that the only language Outlaws understand, is being hunted and shot like dogs. I don't know why you're after these men, but I reckon if you've been chasing after 'em from Blackfoot County, you must have a pretty damn good reason for wanting to spill their blood."

"It's like you say there, Joe. Shooting someone now-a-day's isn't as cut and dry as it used to be five years ago."

Jake hesitates for a brief moment. Joe

Evans sees the look in Jake's eyes, and he instinctively knows that the man sitting in front of him isn't just after these men for the sheer fun of it.

"Well Joe, to tell you the honest truth, it's a long and sordid story, which I don't like talking about. I made a promise that I'd hunt them all down and make them pay for their crime. I intend to carry out my pledge to my wife."

Joe nods his head and replies, "Believe me when I tell you that I understand better than you might think, Jake. If and when those men do come to town, and your paths cross, I'll turn a blind eye."

Both men exchange long looks, each

busy with their own thoughts on the matter at hand. It's Jake who breaks the silence after a minute or two.

"I don't rightly know what I'm going to do when it comes down to us facing each other over a distance, Joe, and that's the truth. I reckon I'll play it by what Tex Burrows does. He has a more violent nature than me. So, whichever way he deals the cards, I'll handle it at that moment. One thing you gotta know, though. If I don't gun him down in your town's streets, he's still going to pay the price for what he did. Going to trial for murder and Larson, as well as all his other crimes he's committed could also be just as good, coz he'll sure as hell go to the gallows for that."

Joe grins and nods when he replies, "Now we're talking the language I like to hear. Hearing from your own mouth that it might not end in a shoot-out, is all I wanted. I will, however, after hearing your story, expect the worst to happen, so in case it does, it doesn't catch me off-guard. Well, that's it then. Let's hope for the best. How long you plan on staying here in Tombstone?"

"Aw, let's say about a day or two to start with. Depends how things pan out. If nobody's arrived during the time that I'm staying, I'll be on my way. Just bear with me for a couple of days."

A DISH BEST SERVED COLD

FRIDAY, MID-MORNING. Sierra Vista; Cochise County.

The air is crisp, and has a bite to it which was not previously there. The nights are getting longer, and the days shorter. That means less daylight to travel in on horseback.

Tex and Josh ride into town without much notice being taken of the pair. It's a typical mining town, of which a lot have been rising during the last couple of years.

Everybody seems to think that they are going to find their pot of gold at the end of the Rainbow. However, of all the claims staked out, only a few produce good enough diggings to survive and make a decent living.

Mostly, after a couple of months, the
remainder of people divert to farming, others moving on to bigger towns in search of better luck.

The streets are busy, and this suits Tex and his companion, Josh, just fine. It makes everything just so much easier for them. They can blend in, become part of the crowds of people roaming around, and go about picking their targets without anybody suspecting anything.

"Hey, Tex, to our left. Nobody's goin' to notice if we keep an eye on that there spot for a while. We might's well take stock on the law in town, while we're at it."

Tex glances sideways, his eyes immediately focusing on the large board
that reads "American Bank; for the American who believes in tomorrow."

Tex looks over at Josh, and sniggers. He looks pretty nasty with the scar stretching across his whole lower lip and chin, the dark pink color making it stand out even more.

"Let's go have ourselves a drink Josh, talk to some people. It's still early, so the poor sods who're sittin' in the bars, are mostly the town drunks anyway, an' they'll spill the beans on their own mothers for a couple o' drinks. They're gonna tell us what the compliment of Lawmen in this here town is, an' when bankin' day is. For all we know, today might be our lucky day."

Josh's mouth pulls a little to one side as he listens to Tex, approving of this way of thinking. He calls it a smile, though it's nothing more than a mere twitch. It's as if Tex reads his mind. Josh thinks of himself and Tex as two peas in a pod, certain that Tex too, feels that way. In his mind him and Tex are equal, even though the words have not been spoken as such.

"Sure hope so, Tex. I'm gettin' pretty damn tired o' eatin' Beef Jerky an' nothin' else. Ain't had me a decent steak in a while, an' a cold beer would go down swell! Let's get busy."

Dismounting in front of a saloon that has seen much better days, they tether their horses close to the drinking trough and go inside. It's gloomy inside, cigarette and cigar smoke filling the air. About fifteen men are either seated at or close to the proximity of the bar counter, nursing a beer or cheap Whisky.

Another ten or so are seated at various tables in the saloon, not even bothering to look up as Tex and Josh walk towards the bar counter. Tex can't help but notice, and points it out to Josh. Although the saloon is barely standing, the bar counter is made of Oak, and glimmers and shines like a mirror in the smoke-filled, vile smelling room.

"What can I do you for, gentleman? My beers're cold, there's cheap Whisky, and then there's the good stuff. Take your pick, the first round's on the house. That's the tradition around here with newcomers or travelers."

"That's mighty generous of you friend. What'll it be, Josh? Hurry it up will you; I ain't gonna wait all day so you can make up your mind. Bartender, I'll have me a proper double Whisky, no water. Not too much ice either, make it more Whisky than ice, and like I said; see that it's a large one. You can damn well order your own drinks from here on in, Josh. I ain't here to entertain you!"

Tex speaks with vehemence, startling Josh, as it's unexpected. Tex's fast-changing moods scare the hell out of him, and Lord knows what else he's capable of when booze is part of the menu. Josh has never before seen that side of Tex, although he has his ideas of what can be in store not only for him, but also for others.

It can get ugly. For a moment Pete fills a portion of Josh's thoughts, and he wonders where he went to, if he started a new life like he said he was going to. Josh thinks that if there is anyone who will be able to start afresh, it's Pete. "Hey, now hold on there a minute. My mind was occupied there for a while Tex. I ain't expectin' you to spoon feed me like you say, I'm perfectly able to see to myself, I'll have you know. Wonder what became of Pete, d'you think he made it?"

"Now ain't the time or the place to be wonderin' about Pete. He's old enough to look out for himself, in case you haven't noticed. Keep focused to our plan Josh, or everythin'll turn to shit again. I don't plan on getting involved in a shoot-out with the Law again, it attracts too much attention, which is somethin' we can't afford right now. I'm warnin' you, keep your act together."

"Alright, alright. Keep your pants on. Jeez, what's with you these last couple weeks? You're so high-strung you might's well walk a tightrope."

"Shut your trap, Josh. Keep jawbonin' me, and I promise you I'll shut your big mouth for good. Are we clear on that?"

Tex is now facing Josh, and his eyes are mere slits in his face, his breathing irregular. Josh realizes that he's taken it too far with Tex, and subsequently withdraws like the sea from the shore.

"Hell, Tex, didn't mean to upset you. I was just yankin'your chain a little. It's nothin' to get so worked up about. Forget what I said, it don't mean nothin'. Now that there", Josh pointed to a man sitting all by himself, hugging his drink close to him, "looks like someone to chat to, wouldn't you say?"

By admitting defeat, and changing the conversation, Josh manages to shift Tex's anger from him, and replace his anger with curiosity. Frowning, Tex looks at the figure sitting alone at a table, and sums up the position quickly and accurately. He hates to admit it, but he has to come to the same conclusion as Josh, who after all, proves to be an asset to him.

"Yeah, I get your meanin'. He looks like he could be our little chatterbox, if we feed him enough of what he's drinkin'. C'mon, let's go talk to him an' see if he's as fragile as he looks."

The clock tower announces that it's exactly half past three. In another thirty minutes the American Bank will be closing for the day. The drunk in the saloon turns out to be a unique source of information.

After a couple more drinks, Tex and Josh become the best friends he's ever had in his entire sorry excuse for a life. He is known all over as Gus, just Gus. No surname, he's forgotten it more years ago than he can remember.

Doesn't even know his age, although he guesses he could be around fifty or so. Tex mumbles that he looks more like seventy to him. One eye is blind, and stares straight ahead, no matter where he is looking with the other eye, and his clothes are in tatters, the shoes maybe once upon a time recognizable for the purpose they are meant to be used for.

The train will be pulling into the station in another three quarters of an hour, enough time to hold up the bank, and if their timing is right, to board the train just in time as it's getting ready to leave. Tex and Josh are seated comfortably on the boardwalk in front of the bank, each smoking a cigar they bummed off one of the men also drinking in the saloon.

They haven't aroused any suspicion or funny looks up to now, for there are plenty of people lining the boardwalk at this hour. At exactly two minutes to four, as the Bank Manager walks across the floor towards the door to close it for business, Tex and Josh are ready.

With brute force, Tex jams his heavy frame into the door, forcing it open with a loud thud against the Banker. Four people are on their way out, when they are forcefully thrown back, falling to the ground. As the Banker is too stunned to move, the door remains open for thirty seconds or so, making lea-way for one of the citizens to quickly flee the scene.

"Shit, Josh, why didn' you stop that man who just ran out here? You know what this means, don't you! It means we're goin' to have to shoot it out with the Law again, an' who knows how many others. You stupid idiot, after I told you to watch the door, you let one person slip right by you to sound the alarm. We could've been gone an' out in no time, without any complications, but no, you got to follow your own damn fool-ass ideas. You, Banker, get me what I came here for, and make it snappy! I ain't got all day to stand here and exchange friendly words. As a matter of fact, if you're not back with the money in sixty seconds, I'm goin' to blow a hole in you the size o' the Grand Canyon! An' you there on the ground, you'd better be quiet as mice."

"Tex, I think you'd better come have a look out the window right away."

Tex immediately recognizes fear in Josh's voice, and hurries over to where the latter is standing. Tex's stomach gives a jolt, and nearly turns upside down. He didn't expect a welcoming committee!

"Hell, I was afraid of this. How the hell you think we're goin' to get out of this mess? You'd better help me think of a plan here Josh. This is your fault after all, so get the little brains you have left, working! I ain't planning on dyin' here today, so whatever it is you come up with, better work, or I'll have your guts for garters."

That said, Tex turns and strides towards the Banker, who has returned with four medium sized white bags, and lays them on the ground.

"Open 'em up four eyes, I wanna see the dough."

With trembling fingers, the Banker opens the bags as instructed, and after a quick look inside, Tex is satisfied with the findings.

"Ok, tie them again, mister Banker. You can thank your lucky stars there's cash in them bags. I'm feelin' lucky today, so I'll let you live for now. Now ain't that nice of me? I know what we're gonna do Josh, to get us out of here."

"Well, whatever it is you have in mind, we'd better do it now, or die tryin'. They're mighty close an' closin' in."

"You're takin' one hostage, an' I'll be takin' our Banker here to accompany me on our way out. He's been so helpful, I wanna really give him the opportunity to show us his gratitude for lettin' him live. Take that fat lady over there. Looks like she has plenty of weight to throw around this hick of a town. What's your husband do, sweetie; yeah, you fatso!"

The Banker intervenes at this point, stepping forward.

"It isn't very polite to speak to a lady like that, mister. Around here we don't tolerate manners like yours. If you hand back the bags of money, and let these innocent citizens go free, I give you my word of honor that I will see to it that neither of you spend a very long time behind bars, which would be the case should you decide to go through with this plan of madness of yours."

Without saying a word, Tex quickly steps forward and hits the Banker with the muzzle of his six-gun across the face, leaving a gaping wound gushing blood all over the floor.

"You've just shortened your life tryin' to be a hero. How stupid can you get? I don't need you nor anybody else to give me free advice, got it?"

Josh sees that things are going to take a turn for the worst, especially for him and Tex. He interrupts urgently.

"Tex, you can see to him later. Right now, we gotta get away outta this town."

Tex grabs hold of the Banker, and dragging him by the collar, orders the fat lady to get up.

"Josh, grab a hold of her, let's get the hell outta here. We can use these two as shields, an' I'll stake my life they won't shoot once they see us bein' covered by two o' their townsfolk."

Tex pushes Josh and his hostage out the door, shouting at the mob that have assembled a way's off from the bank.

"We got two of your citizens wrapped up with us, so if you wanna go ahead an' endanger their lives by shootin' at us, go right ahead. That'll give me an' my pardner here enough time to take a couple of you hero's with us. Your bank manager's goin' to bleed to death by the way, if you don't let us pass peacefully."

Josh is waiting on the boardwalk, using the fat lady as his shelter. There's no chance of him being hit.

"C'mon, Tex, let's make a run for it. The horses ain't that far, just across the street man."

A man steps forward from the crowd, his hand on his gun; ready to draw. He has a five point star pinned to a leather jacket on his chest.

"You ain't gettin' past me mister, even if it means me alone against the two of you. I'm the Law in this town, and I don't intend to let any of my citizens get in harm's way. So you might just as well give it up right here and now. You're two against myself and all the rest of the men standing behind me, just waiting on my order to let loose and riddle you with bullets. Do the right thing here, friend, and hand those people and the moneybags over to me. I'll see you don't sit too long."

Tex squints at the man speaking. His breathing is hard and irregular, and Josh knows what's coming when he notices the look on Tex's face.

Before Josh can heed Tex not to do anything hasty, Tex shoves his gun in the Banker's ribs and squeezes the trigger. It happens so unexpectedly that Tex gains the necessary timeframe that he had in mind when they exited the bank and he saw the amount of people they'll have to face.

With the sound of the gunshot still hanging in the air, Tex levels his gun and squeezes off another shot. It hits the Sheriff high in the shoulder, spinning him around like a bobbin. The gates of Hell open up. Suddenly rifles and guns fire from everywhere.

Bullets are whizzing dangerously close to Tex and Josh as they flee the spot where they have just been standing, sig-sagging their way across the street to where their horses are tethered. Both men jump with practiced ease into the saddles, their horses already at a gallop.

Passing the group of men who have been shooting at them, Tex is almost on top of the Sheriff, who has not stood up yet from where he's fallen. Tex lifts his gun and squeezes off two more shots at point blank range. Both shots find their targets.

The first bullet thuds into the Sheriffs chest, while the second bullet smashes through his teeth, blowing away the back of his head. He crumples into a heap, blood gushing from the mortal wounds he's been dealt, covering the ground around him in a crimson red river.

Josh knocks two others of the group of townsmen to the ground with good placed shots as him and Tex speed away, taking the route due North, spurring their horses as hard as they can. The people of Sierra Vista are dismayed.

In a time-span of four to five minute/s they have been left without someone to lead them lawfully, their banker and two other fellow-men are dead, and they've been robbed of all the money in the bank. It takes a little time before the group of people can be calmed down.

CHAPTER TEN

Jake has been in Tombstone for three days, one day more than he has anticipated staying, and he has a gut instinct that the two outlaws aren't going to show up. The law in this town is too tight. It's a town known for its tough Lawmen, and people around here have already began to stand up for their rights.

Outlaws travelling the Owl-hoot are not welcome in these parts any longer. On the morning of the fourth day, Jake walks over to the Marshall's office, where he finds Joe Evans bent over a stack of paper work. The Marshall looks up as Jake enters after a quick knock on the door.

"Hey Jake, how're you doing? By the looks of it, I'd say you're on your way out, right? If that's how it is, I'll be sorry to see you go. I've become quite used to having that ugly mug of yours around town. Come and sit down, have a cup of coffee."

"I'm doin' great, Joe, although I'd hoped that those two scum bags would've shown up by now. I reckon they're headed somewhere else, so I'll have to saddle up an' go lookin' for 'em again. He keeps stayin' one pace ahead of me, but I reckon we'll cross paths again, likely sooner than later. I can't shake the feelin' that he's closer now than I've ever been to him in months. That drives me nuts, I'm tellin' you, but I know I have to keep a level head on this. How far's that coach distributin' them sketches of Tex Burrows? Heard any news on that so far?"

Joe shakes his head and says "No luck on that one so far Jake; unfortunately. Best we can do is sit and hope he goes someplace where a poster was dropped off, and somebody recognizes him. I wish you all the luck in the world on this one. It's quite a pinch, and I wouldn't want to stand in your boots, to tell you the God's honest truth. Where you headed? Maybe I can be of some help in that department, seeing as you've never travelled these parts. The towns further up North around this State are small, and easy to miss. Let's see what we come up with."

Joseph Evans gets up and walks around his desk to where an enormous map of the State of Arizona is pinned to a board. Joe calls Jake closer when he indicates to a spot on the map, saying "Come have a look here Jake. We're down South here, at this point. Down here is where those outlaws robbed the bank and killed a Sheriff. Now if I were them, I wouldn't come here either, cause the law's too tight, and the chances of them getting caught are much bigger than if they would go to any of the smaller towns. Here's
what I would do if I were you."

Jake follows Joe's finger as he runs his finger along the Counties.

"I'd carry on to Benson from here. Once in Benson, find out from the Sheriff there whether they've had any strangers hanging around the last couple of days or so. I'll give you the poster that we had printed. It's gonna make things just so much easier for you."

Jake has, in the meantime followed the towns on the map, and mouths his thoughts.

"Yeah, I think from Benson I'll follow the trail straight North-Westerly into Pima County and make for Tucson. I should be there in about half a day's travel-lin', don't you think?"

"I'm sure half a day's reasonable. You could get there a lot sooner, but that would mean you'd have to push your horse to its limits. When you arrive in Tucson, go see the U.S. Marshall, he's a friend of mine. His name's Bill Paxton. He's fair, and hates outlaws. If there's anybody that can help you, it'll be him, and if your man's in his town, he'll come down on him like a ton of bricks, of that you can be sure."

"Thanks, Joe, I'll be sure to make contact with these lawmen. Ok well, that's it then. I'll go an' speak to your friend the Marshall an' see if he can shed some light. I'd be obliged if you could send him a cable an' tell him I'll be comin' his way."

The two men shake hands, and Jake goes back to the hotel to get his belongings together for the trip that lies ahead of him, come the following morning.

XXX

Jake goes up the steps leading to the Sheriffs office. After a hefty knock on the door and a "Come inside, the door's open if you wanna talk," Jake opens the door and enters. The Sheriff stares at Jake as he enters the office and strides towards the large desk that fills the entire one corner. Jake offers his hand.

"Afternoon Sheriff. Name's Jake Hudson. I just arrived from Tombstone, an' I thought it would be wise to pop in here. Got this here poster with me. I'd like to know if you've maybe seen this man around here. Been chasin' him across four States. Just missed him an' a partner of his down in Sierra Vista. They robbed the bank there just before the train pulled into town, killed the Sheriff and three citizens."

The Sherriff listens very intently to Jake's story, playing with a toothpick in his mouth. He rises from behind his desk, and sticks out a calloused hand.

"How do you do Jake; been expecting you. The stagecoach driver, who delivered the exact same poster to me three days ago, mentioned you'd most probably be around here some time or other. Kept my eyes peeled these last couple o' days, but didn't see anybody around my town resembling this fellow. By the way, I'm Jeff Dorsey."

"Hell, this man's like a ghost. He pops up like a virus, makes trouble, an' then he disappears for a while. Thought he might head for a small town an' lay low for a while, 'but it looks like his brain works the opposite way."

"Well, If I had a large amount of cash, I'd rather go to a city. He can buy himself a lot of pleasure with money, and he'd be right at home blending in with all the big spenders. Why don't you spend the night here in Benson, and carry on tomorrow morning with your search? Besides, it's going to be dusk pretty soon, no use in getting back on the trail now. You can have the bed here in the office if you're not too particular. There ain't anybody in the cells, and my deputy's sick, so the bed's vacant."

"Thanks for the generous offer, Jeff. I'll just go an' have myself a good dinner, then I'll come back and take you up on your offer."

xxx

Rays of bright yellow sunshine fill the office when Jake awakens to find the Sheriff standing over the coffee pot, brewing it to bring out the full aroma of the roasted beans. Yawning, and wiping his eyes as he does so, Jake gets up and walks over to where the Sheriff is stan-

ding with a mug in his hand.

"Morning. Left you to sleep a little, you looked bushed. Slept well, I trust? That bed's not the best there is, but it beats sleeping on the ground, doesn't it? Coffee?"

"Yeah, thanks."

Jake takes the mug offered to him by Jeff Dorsey, thankful to wet his dry throat. He suspects that his dry throat may have been caused by a whole lot of snoring on his part. His hair is wet at the temple, so Jake guesses that some drooling is also involved. He is disgusted in himself. This has never happened to him before.

Jake washes the grit out of his eyes and pulls his fingers through his hair.

"Thanks for the free bed and break-fast, Jeff. I'll be on my way now."

Jeff Dorsey opens a cupboard and takes out some supplies. He hands these to Jake, saying "Take this, Jake. I know you ain't got time to drop by the grocer and get supplies. I'll get some more later on. For cryin' out loud, keep your money. This stuff ain't worth a dime. Go on, get! You're wasting valuable time. Keep well, and best of luck with whatever crosses your path."

Jake walks over to the Livery, saddles Jet and with a last wave of his hand as he passes the Sheriff's office, Jake leaves Benson behind in a cloud of dust.

TEX TURNS IN THE SADDLE after he reins in his horse, waiting for Josh to catch up with him. In the distance he can see puffs of dust rising into the air. He knows what that means, and is aggravated that he has not been able to shake the Posse now for almost two hours.

Tex knows that they've gone too far too many times, and shooting and killing the Sheriff and another citizen, has sealed their fates. It doesn't look as if this mob will simmer down. His anger flaring up, Tex decides that if Josh wants to ride alongside him, he will have to start moving his ass if he wants to keep up. He isn't about to wait on Josh like Royalty.

"C'mon you lazy bum, let's get a move on! You see those dust clouds down yonder? It's the Posse still chasin' us, an' if they catch up with us, we're dead meat! I ain't tellin' you again, if you can't keep up, I'm leavin' you all to yourself to fend for. I ain't baby-sittin' you any longer, an' I don't intend on gettin' caught with you either, coz if that bunch of vigilantes catch up with you, I promise you you're goin' to rot away in a cell in some Godforsaken prison, or worse still; they'll stretch your neck at the end of a rope. That ain't my idea of fun."

"Yeah okay, I get the picture, Tex. Damn it all, this horse is worse'n a mule! It don't have no spunk left, just listen to its uneven breathin'. Sounds like its goin' to drop dead or somethin'. What you want me to do with this horse; shoot it? That'll be a solution, coz what do I ride with then?"

"Don't sass me Josh. I ain't in the mood for your brainless jawbonin'. Just make up your mind, and be quick about it. If you ain't ready within the next five minutes, I'm leavin' you behind, got that?"

While Tex and Josh have their conversation, Tex doesn't notice just how quickly the Posse has gained on them. When Tex calls on Josh to mount, he looks towards where he's last seen dust clouds drift up, and is caught by surprise. By quick estimation, Tex sees that the Posse is only about five miles behind them, and closing in fast. Headway has to be made now, or never.

"Whoa, stretch your legs pardner. It's time to rise to the challenge and show me what you're made of! You ready Josh, coz I ain't stoppin' till I'm sure we've lost em."

Josh also looks back, and immediately catches on to Tex's meaning. The gap between them and their pursuers have closed tremendously fast. This seems to inspire Josh to get a move-on. He gets his horse to move a lot faster than before. They have to ride and ride fast, or die. The latter is not a negotiable

negotiable consideration to either one of them.

With this in mind, they spur their horses and let them run at their own will. The horses don't hold anything back. The ground flies by, and quickly Josh's horse again sags back. Its coat glistens with perspiration, and foam gathers at its mouth, with his nostrils that flare wide.

It's eyes are wild and rolling in its head. Then it happens so suddenly that neither Josh nor Tex sees it coming. Josh's horse slams into the ground like a Tornado, actually making a hole where it falls in a majestic cloud of dust.

"You go on ahead, Tex! I'll catch up

with you, just need to rest my horse a mite, an' give him some water. Think he's had too little to drink, looks like he's a little dehydrated. I'm goin' to take him into some shade by the river, let him just cool off an' have some water. Soon's you can say six, I'll be right behind you again. If you don't see me, wait for me in Tucson!"

Tex doesn't even look back as he speeds on, not bothered whether Josh will be alright or not. It's now survival of the fittest, and Tex decides that he won't be pulled down by Josh's weakness. He's on his own now; thank goodness for that. There's nobody who can hold him back now, which is more than Josh is able to say.

Josh knows that he either has to get his horse up and going, or stay here longer than necessary and risk being captured. Worse even, that angry mob of townsmen can decide to shoot and kill him on the spot when they catch up with him. He has a sudden attack of goose bumps at this thought.

"C'mon you useless critter. Lift your bony ass and get us out of here. You hear me? We're both goin' to die if we stay here for much longer. Those men back yonder mean business, damn it!"

Josh splashes more water over his horse's body and head, and pours some of the life giving mineral into his hat, holding it so his horse can drink. Feeling the coolness of the water on his body, and smelling the water, he feebly lifts his head and drinks thirstily. With an awe-inspiring lunge, Josh's horse manages to stumble to its legs, still very unstable, but willing to try its best to serve its master.

Josh leads his horse to a small river just off the trail, leaving it to walk waist-deep into the cool water. He can literally see the strength flow back into his horse as it gulps mouths full of the life-sustaining delicacy. Josh whistles, and waits as his horse comes trotting back, now fully revived after some forty minutes' rest and enough water.

Josh puts the saddle back on, and is busy tying his bedroll to the back of his saddle, when he becomes aware of the thunder of hoof beats not far off. He quickly mounts, steering his horse back onto the trail and gives it a lashing with the reins.

Quickly they're travelling at high speed, but not before Josh hears a loud scream rise up from behind him. Anxiously looking over his shoulder, he sees that five horsemen are closing in on him at break-neck speed, spreading out in a semicircle, their rifles already out and ready to fire.

Unless a miracle happens to come along, Josh knows that he's done for. The odds against him are too great to beat, but he won't go down without giving them a run for their money, of that they can be sure.

"Nobody's goin' to take me alive, I'll die with my boots on!", Josh thinks to himself as he pulls out his six-gun from its holster. With practiced skill, he lets go of a couple of well-placed shots. One of the shots finds its mark, flinging the pursuer out of his saddle to bite dust.

Another's horse stumbles and falls when the pursuer goes down, leaving three to reckon with. They have already fallen back a little, not ready for the sudden gun-battle that has started without any warning.

"Take that! That oughta keep you off my back for a while, you cockroaches! Didn't expect me to come out shootin', did you? Well, you ain't seen nothin' yet. I'm just gettin' started!" Josh yells at them.

Josh leaves his pursuers behind as he had hoped he would, and just as these thoughts race through his mind, he feels his horse stumble. Then he hears the loud crack of a rifle.

Without a doubt he knows that his horse has been hit, because he can feel the energy seep out of his horse. He also has trouble running, and slows down to a walk within a few meters after being hit by the bullet.

Dismounting, Josh curses under his breath. What more can go wrong for him, hasn't he suffered enough these past months? A quick inspection brings him to the cause of his horse's discomfort. It's been shot high in the back quarter of the rump, the bullet lodging itself deep into the thick muscle. The wound isn't bleeding profusely, but Josh knows that the horse won't be able to last for a prolonged period of time before it collapses.

JAKE IS GRATEFUL FOR the supplies that Jeff Dorsey gives him before his departure from Benson. He's been running a little low on a few items, such as canned food, coffee and sugar, and a few other necessities. The sun is like a giant fireball, scorching man and beast in its path.

Fortunately, Tucson isn't too far away from Benson; half a day's ride will get him there in good time before darkness falls. Jake plans on getting himself settled in for the evening and getting everything arranged first, before going to see the US Marshall in the morning. Riding at an easy pace, Jake enters Tucson just as the sun begins to set, and dusk crawls over the horizon with grey fingers.

Reining in in front of The Palace hotel, Jake unsheathes his Winchester and unties his bedroll, then goes up the four steps onto the boardwalk, letting his gaze quickly take in the surroundings. Approving of the area, Jake opens the glass door leading to the inside of the hotel, and steps into the foyer.

Walking straight to the huge desk that runs the entire length of the lobby, Jake is met by an elderly bald man, resting a pair of spectacles on the bridge of his nose. He is immaculately dressed in a crisp, clean uniform.

"Good evening sir. Can I help you?", he politely enquires from Jake.

"Yes, please. I'd like a room and a stable for my mount."

"Certainly, sir. If you'll follow me? Charlie, take the gentleman's belongings, and show him to his room. You can sign the register later, sir."

Jake doesn't feel like returning at a later stage, and asks to sign the register immediately. The clerk who assigns Jake's room, isn't very talkative. He just gives Jake a fake smile and unpleasant stare, before pushing a thick ledger towards him.

"Sign there, please. It'll be ten dollars for the night."

Jake hands him twenty dollars, an indication that he will be staying for two nights. The clerk hands Charlie the porter,keys, who leads Jake up the stairs and turns left into a long corridor. He unlocks the door of number seven, and fidgets with the keys, obviously nervous.

Jake takes the keys from him, and without any effort, opens the door to the room. It's large and luxuriously furnished, with its own private bathroom. Jake's bedroll and saddlebags are put down on the bed, after which Jake tips the porter five dollars.

"For another five, see that my horse gets stabled and well fed. Tell the Liveryman I'll come and fix up with him tomorrow morning. Think you can handle that?"

Jake looks at the porter question-ingly.

"Why yes, of course sir. No problem. Just tell me which horse is yours, and I'll see he's taken care of."

"Be careful, my horse is a little wild, and he likes to bite. He's standing out front, an' you can't miss him. He's velvet black with a snow white chest and hooves, an' he responds to the name Jet."

"'That's fine sir, don't you worry none. I'm used to all sorts o' horses, grew up on a horse ranch just outside o' town. Horses like me, and the feelings mutual, so your horse's in good hands."

Jake slips him another five dollars as promised. He likes the youngster, for he's eager to work and please, and shows promise to excel in whatever he should decide to take up for a career. Washing up quickly, Jake changes into a clean shirt and goes downstairs to the restau-

rant where he will have dinner.

Tucson is a rapidly growing town, bursting from its seam as development knows no bounds. It's clear that civilization is taking over more and more every day. Jake looks in amazement at the amount of people who go about their business. He takes a table at the window, so he can have a clear view of the street. It's a slim chance, but Jake hopes that he will run into Tex Burrows in Tucson.

If his partner-in-crime is with him, and has a beef with Jake, well, then that will be that. Tex's partner will have to stand in line with Tex for what will be handed out and not any less.

Jake has already placed his order, and is waiting for his beer to arrive, when his eye catches a quick glimpse of a recognizable face in the crowd across the street. Then it's gone. Jake looks for a second time, but can't discern the same face he saw mere seconds before.

"You must be seein' ghosts, Jake ole buddy. Either you're tired, or you're wishin' so hard to see one o' them skunks you're after, that your eyes are playin' tricks on you", Jake speaks softly to himself. He knows that he'll be able to recognize Tex, even if he's also grown a beard, because of the scar on his lower lip and chin.

Jake has heard talk that it's quite

distinguishable, and stands out like a sore thumb. As he thinks about this, his dinner arrives. After saying grace, Jake ploughs into his dinner, enjoying the meal and cleaning the plate with one last sweep of a fresh bread roll.

Satisfied, Jake decides to call it an evening and retire to his hotel room. His first stop come morning will be the Marshall, who must be expecting him any time soon.

XXX

"Mornin'; you Bill Paxton? Deputy Marshall by the name of Joe Evans in Tombstone said to come see you when I arrive in Tucson. Name's Jake Hudson. Sorry to barge in on you this early in the mornin'."

Bill Paxton looks up from where he is seated behind his desk, a deep frown burrowing a crease in his forehead.

"It's absolutely fine. Come on in and take a seat; I'll be with you in just a minute. Been expecting you. Joe sent me a telegram saying to look out for you. Explained something about a couple outlaws you're chasing, but I expect you'll fill me in with some more detail. Sit yourself down so long; be with you in a minute."

Jake sits down and waits patiently for Bill Paxton to finish his paper work. It takes only a couple of minutes for the Marshall to complete his task at hand. He pushes the papers away from him and focu-ses his attention on Jake.

"Okay, Jake; let's hear the story. I'm nosy as hell!"

Looking over his desk at Jake, Bill Paxton can see that it isn't easy for Jake. He gives him time. Jake looks up and right into the eyes of Bill Paxton. He begins his story.

"Yeah, it's a hell of a story. Here's where it all started ...

Marshall Bill Paxton listens intently to Jake's story, every now and again nodding his head as indication that he's following Jake. Jake continues and Bill Paxton leaves Jake to finish his story.

"That's the story behind my journey,

Bill. Every time I get close to them, they make a run for it, as if they know I'm onto 'em."

Bill Paxton shakes his head and cusses when he says, "I'd also be pissed as hell. You have reason to take vengeance, Jake. Rest assured, I'm backin' you on this one. You still ridin' under the badge?"

Jake shakes his head in denial.

"Sorry to say that I'm not, Bill. Gave up my badge when I took off after Tex Burrows."

"You mean to tell me that there are only two left of a gang of eleven Outlaws, and you've been lucky enough to escape death up to now? Well, hell, then it has to be a sure sign that these men have to be brought to justice by you. Chasing after them for this long and enduring all that you have, gives you the right to own their asses. I sure as hell ain't gonna stand in your way when you find 'em, on that I'll give you my word. Also, if there's anything else you need some help with, you just holler the word."

"Thanks, Bill, appreciate you understandin'. Here's a photo-print of both men I'm after. I sure would be glad if your Deputies could just keep their eyes open, an' when they spot any of these two men, to just give me a shout."

"I can imagine that it must be an all-

consuming hatred that haunts a man like a ghost. I aim to turn a deaf ear and a blind eye. It's a pity the West ain't what it used to be a couple years ago, when you could take a life for a life, and square the odds. Well, I suppose times have to change, and there's nothing we can do about it, except go along."

"You can say that again, Bill. Once I've completed my journey, I'm hangin' up my guns for good. Ain't no place for 'em in the future. I've had enough of spilling blood. Well, I'll be seein' you a little later on, I guess. Right now there're a few things I need to buy, then I plan to do some scoutin' around town."

CHAPTER ELEVEN

Tex lashes his horse with the reins He has no remorse for leaving Josh all by himself. Tex's motto has always been everyone for himself when danger lurks. He has always had to look out for himself, since he can remember. Tex thinks back to his childhood days, if one can call it that.

His father is a no-good, worthless and jobless drunk. He returns home at night after being out all day "looking" for a job, as drunk as a skunk, and angry at the world. One of his many pass-time's is to slap Tex's mother around. Tex is too young to protect his mother from the vicious blows that leave her near cripple and beat to a pulp.

Tex always receives a terrible beating after his father finishes with his mother. He tries to fend off the blows, but in doing so, only inflames his father's rage. He is kicked like a dog when he falls, and on more than one occasion, a few of his ribs are broken during the scuffle.

Tex shares this life with his mother until his sixteenth birthday, when he puts an end to their existence of hell. He secretly lifts some weights and exercises his body, making it tough and resilient, and also gains muscle along the way.

He is still too young for it to make a difference, but as the years pass Tex's body becomes so strong and resilient against the fierce attacks by his father, that he no longer suffers from the aftermath of violent beatings.

Tex's father is also too intoxicated every time he beats up on Tex and his mother to notice the change in his son's physique. When assaulted thus for the umpteenth time during her marriage, and certain to be killed this time round, Tex has had enough.

He stands up to his father and challenges him to finish the fight with him instead. He stands his ground like a true champion against the ferocious onslaught, taking a couple of blows that nearly puts him down.

One lucky punch saves the day for both him and his mother. Tex pulls the punch from way back, puts all his weight behind it, and lets it smack home. The instant it finds its mark, Tex knows it's a sitter. His father's knees buckle as he stumbles backwards. He trips over the coffee table and hits the floor with a sickening thud, splitting his skull in two.

There is no inquest into the death of Tex's father, as everybody knows him to always be drunk and disorderly. The doctor defines his death as an accident while intoxicated. Tex stays with his mother until her passing, three years later. After burying her, Tex decides to pack up and hit the trail.

He becomes a cowpuncher, and is quite good at it. After working on several ranches, he hitches the job as Ranch foreman at the SquareT Ranch, where he's Foreman for nine months before the incident with Jake Hudson. Tex is jerked back to reality by the sound of gunshots.

Tex hears the gunshots after leaving Josh, and also distinguishes the rifle shot shortly after. Then, all of a sudden, it's quiet, but Tex doesn't for one moment think of turning back. He heads for Tucson as fast as he can let his horse run. Deciding to head for a large town with a lot of inhabitants, is his only way out now.

He isn't known in the large towns in any of the Western States or in the far North-West, because there are too many people up that way nowadays. Besides, how will anybody know him to be an Outlaw when they see him?

Nobody has a picture of him, nor is there any reward on his head. This thought makes him feel safe, and after riding hard for another couple of miles, he holds back on the reins, giving his horse a bit of a breather by slowing his pace to an easy trot.

Daybreak arrives as a welcome interlude, for Tex has travelled right through the night in order to get to Tucson, and is now saddle-sore and tired to the bone. He's been in the saddle now for too long this time round. He decides to spend most of the day indoors and sleep his tiredness off.

The only thing he will do before that, will be to have himself a huge breakfast, washed down with a beer or two. As is his luck, there's no Deputy around when Tex enters town. Everything is quiet, with only a few chickens here and there in the streets.

Tex hardly ever leaves his horse at a Livery, for he never knows when he will need his horse in a hurry. This time is no different. He goes down the street and, passing one of the side streets, sees a seedy-looking hotel, and decides to have a look.

Dismounting, Tex enters the lobby, which is dark and gloomy. The night-shift clerk is sleeping with his head on his arms, stretched out in front of him. His snoring fills the entire lobby. He is definitely a sound sleeper.

Tex smashes his gun-butt down hard on the desk next to the clerk's ear. The noise is so loud, that the clerk sits bolt upright, his sleep forgotten, and clutches at his chest. His eyes are wide

open, his mind working in overdrive.

"What the hell you do that for? I was just restin' my eyes for a bit, no need to get riled up about it, friend. Jeez, all you had to do was ask. By the way, everybody comes along this way, knows that they only need to sign in the ledger and take the keys to the room they want. I check the register a little later, see who's signed it, and collect the money that they've left in the register after signing it. Easy as pie. Now you wanna come and mess things up around here. Don't be like that, friend."

Tex looks displeased as he stares at the man.

"I ain't your friend, and don't make me tell your boss you were sleepin' on the job. Now, I want a room, pronto. I'll give you the money for the room later, when the bank opens up, alright? Good, I'm glad we understand one another. Is there something to eat in this shithole you call a hotel? I need to get some food. Can you fix it? Good, if you can, get it sent up to my room, it'll be better. And I don't want to be disturbed, I'm goin' to have myself some shut-eye, got it?"

The clerk shakes his head in bewilderment. This guy is really a little bonkers, one can see it in his eyes, and hear it in the way that he talks, no manners at all. The clerk sums Tex up as being crazy and rude.

Maybe he has to report this stranger to the Marshall. The clerk takes a last look at Tex, and decides against this last notion of his. He doesn't feel like making an enemy out of this man in front of him; he looks as dangerous as a rattlesnake.

"It's alright, man. You go on up to your room, I'll see the cook sends you a nice breakfast, and a pot of coffee."

Tex starts up the stairs, when he turns back.

"Oh, yeah, before I forget. My horse is standin' out front, tied to the pole. Put him up in a stable an' give him some'ing to eat. I'd prefer you to keep my existence a secret for now, also that I'm stayin' here at your hotel. Just in case there're some nosy questions, you know. I don't want it to get all nasty."

That being said, Tex grins, showing off his uneven yellow-stained teeth. His breath reeks of stale tobacco, sending the clerk reeling back to stay out of reach of the sickening smell.

Tex is unaware of the clerk's gaze that follows him all the way to the top of the stairs, disgust written all over it. There have been plenty a character who've come waltzing in here, looking for a place to bed down, but none equals this one, that's for sure. He'll bet all he has that this man means bad news and big trouble. Just then the clerk decides that he isn't going to show up for work that evening.

After getting some shut-eye, he'll walk on over to the Marshal's office, and report what has happened here this morning. He's sure the Marshal will want to know about this scaly guy just pitching up in town, and then choose the seediest-looking place to rest his bones.

Yeah, it doesn't make no sense at all. Looks like he has something to hide. Tex looks like a real hard case to the clerk, who doesn't want to be around when the Marshal comes to investigate this guy; just in case bullets start flying around. Dodging bullets isn't a favorite pass-time of the clerk. Shaking his head, he walks out the lobby and into the fresh morning air.

Jake goes about his business in a few shops, getting himself some new shirts and denims, as well as a pair of new boots. His boots are scuffed and tearing at the seams. Jake also fills up on his canned food, and a fresh new rope. He then goes around to the Livery to see how Jet has settled in, and is pleased to see that the stable hand has given Jet first-class treatment.

Jet whinnies excitedly and snorts loudly when he sees Jake approaching his stable, stomping on the ground with his hooves and bobbing his head up and down, an indication that he wants out of the stables.

"Now, now, pardner; that ain't no way a gentleman behaves himself. I'm payin' good money so you can stay here, so you might's well enjoy it. I reckon we'll be takin' the trail again come tomorrow, that's if nothin' else happens in the meantime to change the deck of cards. Reckon we gotta be a little patient, heh? Well, I tell you, I got this here feelin' in my gut that we're goin' to be lucky this time round, Jet. I just know it! This thing has to come to a close now, it's been draggin' on for months. Anyway pardner, thanks for listenin'. See you tomorrow when we ride outta here, with or without Tex Burrows."

Just as Jake crosses the street towards the saloon for a beer, Bill Paxton calls out to him. Waiting for the Marshall to catch up with him, Jake is curious as to what the Marshall wants from him. They spoke only a couple of hours before, and by the way he's walking, he seems quite anxious.

"Jake, wait up! You're a difficult guy to track down. I've been looking all over for you. I might have something for you, or it might just be nothing. The night-shift clerk who works over at old Abe's, came and told me an interesting story last night. Forgot all about it, until about half an hour or so ago, when the clerk asked me whether I'd gone by the hotel to have a look-see at the stranger he'd told me about. Now, according to him, a stranger came in at the break of dawn yesterday morning. A scruffy looking dude; trail worn and smelling of stale tobacco. Then there's this piece of information I find real interesting, and it has something to do with what you told me about one of the guys you're looking for. Apparently this stranger has a nasty scar on the lower half of his jaw. He spent the whole of yesterday and last night in his room, according to the clerk who worked last night. I just come from there right this minute, and he ain't there, which means he's probably out on the streets or in one of the saloons having a good time and looking things through."

Jake feels the hair in the nape of his neck stand erect, and he gets goose bumps at the announcement of this news flash. Bill Paxton immediately sees the change in Jake's eyes and stature, only then realizing the extent of damage that has messed up his life.

"Take it easy, Jake. No need to rush headlong into things. I've notified my Deputies to go out and see if they can find this guy. When they spot him, they'll come straight to me and report his where-a-bouts. Don't worry, they have instructions not to confront or try and arrest him. If it's him, he's all yours, you have my word on that."

"Appreciate all you're doin', Bill. Chances are he won't even recognize me before it's too late, coz he ain't seen me in months, an' I've grown me this here short beard. He doesn't know me by this look. Just the thought of me being so close makes my heart race. At last he's so close I can almost touch him."

"Let's get off the street, coz if he is around town, we don't want him seeing you talking to me. He might just recognize you if he's forced to look hard enough at your face."

With Bill in the lead, Jake follows him into the Marshall's office, taking a seat in the chair that Bill indicates to. He places himself behind his desk, legs stretched out in front of him, his feet resting on the desk. From the office they have a clear view of everybody coming and going in the streets of the town.

"Now ain't this better than standing out there in the street in this blazing sun? Hell, I can even order us each a beer from the hotel if you want one. The point is; I just think we can observe better from out of my office without being spotted by any unwelcome guests."

"Yeah, you're right. My thinking seems to clog up when I hear that man's name; all rationality goes flying out the window. That's goin' to cause me some problems if I don't watch it. You reckon he'll dare to come into this part of town?"

"I reckon so. Why wouldn't he? There ain't no reason for him to suspect that anything's wrong, or that we're tailing him coz we're aware of who he is and that he's here. According to him, he's safe. What he plans on doing is spending some of that dough he stole, coz he ain't ever had so much money at any one time in his life. I can stake my life on that. He's going to pay big money for a couple of dance-hall girls, and they all talk amongst each other, so sooner or later we'll hear where he's at."

"Hope you're right, Bill. I'd hate to lose him now that he's within reach, and he doesn't even know that I'm right under his nose, just waitin' to pounce on him. Wonder whether that other pardner of his has joined him, or if he's taken off by himself?"

Jake receives no answer from Bill Paxton, for it's a rhetorical question, actually just a thought which has been uttered aloud. He points to a man crossing the street, obviously in a hurry to get where he's going to. Bill Jackson also spots the man.

"That's one of my Deputies. He's in one hell of a hurry, wonder what he came across?"

The Deputy storms into the office, nearly colliding with the wall in his haste.

"Marshall, there's been some new development while we were watching that stranger in town. Me and Ziggy were pub crawlin' like you told us to do from one saloon to the other. When we got to the Golden Nugget Saloon, we were standing talking to the barkeep, when Ziggy noticed this strange fella come in. He nudged me with his elbow, seeing as how he saw him first, and at first I didn't pay him no heed, coz this man doesn't closely resemble the photo you gave us. Then I noticed the scar, but it was hidden beneath a growth of beard stubble about three or four days old."

The Marshall holds up his hand.

"Whoa Jesse, calm down and take a breath. You're likely to faint right here because of a lack of oxygen."

"I'm alright, Marshal. Just a mite winded from running here. Well, like I said, this big fella entered the saloon, and walked to one of the card tables, played a couple rounds and won some pretty good money. Then he walked on over to the back of the saloon, and called for the barkeep to bring him a jug of beer. He sat there all alone and drank his beer, just minding his own business, when another fella who had entered about an hour after him, walked on over and joined him. I could see the huge guy with the scar wasn't expecting company, and nearly drew his gun, when this other guy said something, and they shook hands while they were laughing. Seems he met up with an old friend if I'm not wrong. Ziggy said he'd keep an eye on them, and for me to hurry on over and bring you the news."

Jake is already standing when Bill
Paxton talks.

"Alright Jake, I know you're in a hurry, but don't rush into it. You want a clear head when you walk in there, so you can think straight. The advantage is on your side, coz he doesn't know that you're in town, nor does he know that you know where he's at right this minute. Let's go see what we can do about the situation."

TEX AWAKES INSTANTLY and fully alert to his surroundings. He feels good and refreshed after sleeping for almost the entire day. He doesn't worry much about not being able to sleep again tonight, he never has any problem when it comes to sleeping. What he wants now most of all, is a decent plate of food to replenish his inner strength.

The food that is sent up to his room in the morning, is drab and distasteful, not at all to his liking. Tex feels like bashing the nightshift clerk's head in, but decides to rather keep a low profile. He's had enough trouble with the law to last him a life time. This time round he will settle down, maybe buy himself a nice piece of land and a few hundred head of prime beef, seeing as how he now has the money to do it.

Josh still has to get his share of the loot, but if he doesn't show up after three days, Tex decides that he'll move on. He can't wait here in Tucson forever
and a day.

The nightshift clerk from last night is not on duty again. The new clerk tells Tex that he called in sick. Tex informs the clerk that he wants dinner sent up to his room, and demands that it's good and proper food, not the crap that he had to eat that morning.

"Sick my ass", Tex thinks as he walks away from the desk. "He didn't look sick to me when I came in last night. And he slept while he was supposed to work on top of it all. Lazy critter if you ask me!"

He decides to stay in for the evening, as he also does not have any decent clothing to wear. Tex knows that if he wants to blend in with the rest of Tucson's citizens, he'll have to dress appropriately, otherwise he'll just attract unnecessary attention. That's the last thing he wants. He has to lie low for a while until the heat cools down.

Having made the decision to take it calm, Tex strips of his clothing and lies on the bed; waiting for his dinner to come. He only has a towel draped around his midsection, for he decides to take a bath after he's had dinner. Lucky for him the dreary hotel has a bathroom, something he is very glad about.

At least he'll be able to wash the trail dirt off him and go to bed clean for once. He hasn't had a decent bath in quite a while now. Tex realizes just how bad he has to look at this moment, not to even speak of the smell that clings to him; a sour, gagging smell.

Tex is now becoming very impatient with having to wait so long for his dinner, and is just about to go downstairs to find out what the hold-up is, when there's a knock on the door. With one quick, swift movement, Tex draws his six-gun and takes a stand behind the door.

"Come on in, the door's open!"

The door-handle turns and the door swings open. The person who enters, is wearing a wide brimmed hat. He walks just past the door, when he stops and looks around the room, a puzzled expression on his face. He doesn't have time to elaborate on his thoughts, as the door suddenly shuts behind him, and he feels the cold steel push up against his neck.

"That's far enough! Put the tray on the bed and move away from it."

He does as he is told, and in moving away from the bed, turns sideways. The eyes are enormously big with fright, and he is biting his lower lip. Tex then defines the features as those of a young girl who has brought his food. He immediately holsters his gun.

"Good lord, I'm sorry. I was expectin' a man. I didn't see you were a lady coz of that hat you're wearin'. Didn't see
your hair folded in under the hat."

"O, that's okay. I'm starting to get pretty used to all sorts of characters around here. Been shot once, too. I don't aim to stay here much longer anyways. Hope you enjoy your food, mister; made it myself."

Tex looks hungrily at the girl's curves, longing to hold her in his arms.

"Is that so? Where would I be able to get myself a pretty young thing like yourself to keep me company tonight? Money ain't no problem."

The girl smiles.

"Well, it just so happens that I've gone off duty right this minute, and I happen to be free until tomorrow morning, big fella."

XXX

Tex wakes up feeling tired and spent. His mind races back to last night. That girl had proved to be one helluva hellcat, and had taken Tex by surprise. Anyway, it was worth it. He asks her to go to a clothing shop to get him two decent pairs of trousers and a few shirts, as well as new boots with spurs, giving her some extra cash to spend on herself. That clinches the deal.

Her father is the owner of the hotel, so she says that he is welcome to stay as long as he wants to without any charge. She tells Tex that she can easily manipulate her father into doing just about anything she wants. She is as sweet as honey at an impossible nineteen years of age, and has an insatiable appetite for all the bad things life has to offer.

She returns two hours later with exactly what Tex has asked for. He has to admit that she has quite good taste in clothes as well as boots. He can get used to having her around if he decides to settle down. They have similar likes and dislikes, and he tells her to come back that evening at about eight o'clock. She agrees, and with a last wide smile leaves his room.

Tex has himself another hot bath, lying back in relaxation for almost an hour, soaking up the soapy heat. After washing himself thoroughly, he dresses in his new clothes and boots and goes downstairs, leaving the sordid hotel for the first time in two days. The sun is blazing hot and the glare almost unbearable, and he has to squint his eyes for a while before they become used to the bright glare of light.

Tex walks over to one of the plenty restaurants, nodding his head in friendly greeting to citizens who pass him on his way. Little do they know that he's a two-timing skunk who will just as soon put a bullet in them if the circumstances allow it.

He has a superb breakfast, and then leaves the restaurant, aimlessly wandering around and looking through windows, until he comes to the Golden Nugget Saloon. Entering, his first reaction is to scout the saloon for any Sheriffs or Deputies, an old habit that dies hard, or rather, won't die for as long as Tex lives, for it has become second nature to him.

It has served him well in the past, and has gotten him out of plenty a tight spot. Seeing nothing or nobody suspicious, he walks up to the bar-counter and orders a neat Whisky with crushed ice.

Reveling in the taste and splendor of the luxury that money can now buy him, he enjoys every minute of it. Tex doesn't think that this is the kind of place peace officers will pay frequent visits to, so he feels quite relaxed as he lets his eyes roam the faces that fill the saloon.

Picking a table in the back of the saloon, Tex slowly and purposefully takes his seat. Embedded deep in thought, he never notices the stranger entering the saloon. Tall and skinny, and very trail weary, the stranger lets his eyes dart over the faces in front of him, seeking one in particular. He stares long and hard at Tex, and then notices what he has been looking for.

Casually he walks to where Tex is sitting, and once he arrives at the table, takes out his six-gun and lies it down, muzzle facing forward and the hammer cocked once. Tex's reaction is lightning fast. His gun hand streaks downwards and he draws his gun.

As his gun comes away from its holster, he looks up. Smiling down at him, he recognizes the perfect straight teeth of Josh, and the clear sky-blue eyes. Hastily Tex replaces his gun, getting up off his chair at the same time.

"Josh, you low-life skunk-eatin' dog! Where the hell you been, man? It's been nearly four days since I left you for dead with that posse after us. Didn't think you'd make it out of there alive, but here you are, an' not a scratch on your scrawny yellow hide. It has to be
pure luck."

Both men have a good laugh at this while they shake hands.

"Yeah, I had one hell of a hard time gettin' away from those hellions in the posse. I tell you Tex, they almost had me man. Shot my horse to pieces. I couldn't ride him, had to go into some small little town by the name of Benson to steal me another horse, right out of the Livery stables. Had to knock an old man over the head coz he was askin' too many questions I didn't have answers to. But like you say, here I am, an' I aim to get myself a little bit of pleasure with my part o' the loot. We gotta celebrate this. It ain't everyday a man lives to tell a tale this tall, an' laugh about it."

Jake can't wait to come eye to eye with the man he has come to hate with a passion so deep that it's almost a living thing. Jake's passion to avenge the deaths of his wife and unborn child, is still as strong as the night he'd lost them in that fire. U.S Marshall Bill Paxton feels the change in Jake's demeanor, and the look on his face is as cold as stone.

"C'mon Bill, we can't afford to waste another minute. Now that he's met up with his trail partner again, they might just decide to saddle up and hit the road. Then I'm back to square one! I'm tellin' you, I ain't about to let that happen, no

way!"

Bill can see that Jake is about to throw all caution to the wind, and with his tone rising a notch, he tries to get Jake to calm down.

"Now listen here Jake, and you listen good! I won't allow you to storm into the saloon all boggle-headed and going off the edge, you hear me? This is still my town, and there are other citizens around too, so watch it! I know I said that I'd turn a deaf ear and a blind eye, but only if you don't lose your head. Now's not the time to mess up, you have him pinned down without him knowing it. Use it to your advantage."

Jake calms down a little and pardons himself "I'm sorry Bill, you're right, of course. I lost sight of the big picture there for a moment, but I'm okay now. Let's be on our way, before they give us the slip. Hope you told your Deputies to stand off on this one. Wouldn't want one o' them to get in the middle of a cross-fire an' get hurt on account of my feud."

"Don't worry none, Jake. I've already briefed my men this morning. They know what the situation is, and how to handle it. You're in charge now, so just say the word."

"Thanks, Bill, I appreciate all your help on account of me. You're a good man. Jesse, you lead the way."

With Jesse in the lead, the three men make their way towards the Golden Nugget saloon. It's about two blocks up-town. Five minutes later they near the boardwalk, and go up the four steps to the top of the boardwalk. Jake cautions the other two men to slow down. Calling Jesse closer, Jake whispers to him "Jesse, I want you to go in there as if nothing's the matter. Go up to the bar, and order yourself a drink. While you're waitin' for it, have a look around an' see if scar face an' his friend are still there. Once you've spotted them, just raise your glass like you're wishin' someone well with a toast. Then turn in the direction they're sittin', so I'll know where to look when me an' Bill enter. That'll give me the drop on both of 'em, if any one of them spots me or becomes suspicious before I get the chance to spring a surprise on them. Got that?"

Jesse nods his head "Yeah, I got it. I'll just warn Ziggy that it's about to go down, and to keep his eyes peeled just in case."

Without waiting for an answer from Jake, Jesse quietly slips inside, parting the batwing doors silently. He walks straight to the bar, and Jake can see just enough of him to distinguish that he's looking around the saloon as he walks towards the bar counter.

Doing as Jake requested him to do, he picks up his glass and toasts "someone". Then Jesse turns halfway, his back towards the counter. This is the sign that Jake has waited for. He signals to Bill Jackson, and the both of them enter one after the other.

Fortunately, the lighting is very dim once inside the saloon. This offers comfortable protection from prying eyes. Jake and Bill saunter towards the bar counter, going around to the far side to have a good view of the entire saloon.

Jake lets his glance roam across the room in the direction to where Jesse has turned, and he immediately spots the large bulk of Tex Burrows as he remembers him. He is sitting laid back in his chair at the table that's occupied by himself and another tall but skinny-looking younger man.

These two are the only survivors of the group of eleven outlaws. Tex and his companion, Josh, are in such good moods, because according to the two of them, they're home free, and on top of that, rich as well. They will never have to work another day for as long as they live.

Jake decides that there is no time like the present to make his move, and get whatever is coming, over and done with. He relays his thoughts to Bill, who agrees with him on this. Bill knows that Jake is about to burst out of his seams in a minute or two, as the man he has

managed to hunt down, is in plain sight.

He moves silently with Jake to where the bar ends, leaving him to continue to walk further. Halfway across the floor, it's as if Tex senses that something is very wrong, and silences Josh. The saloon has gone quiet.

Tex finally looks up and stares across the room at Jake. As their eyes meet across the distance, Tex knows with a sickening feeling in his gut that the day of reckoning has arrived.

His hopes that he can put his past behind him, have fallen apart. Tex has to admit to himself, though, when he thinks about it deep down inside, that someday, somewhere, it was bound to catch up with him. Josh sees the look of fear jump into Tex's eyes as he is silenced and he, too, knows. Tex rises from his chair, and holds onto the side of the table with his left hand, resting some of his body weight on it.

Josh slowly turns around and backs away to stand next to Tex. Everybody in the saloon knows what's coming, and hastily make space to stand to one side, so there's no one in the middle of the room. The saloon becomes dead silent; one can hear a fly fart. Jake's voice is like a whiplash in the eerie silence, making Tex start at the sound of it.

"You, Tex Burrows, are responsible for the deaths of my wife, Connie, and our unborn child. I've been huntin' you like the dog you are for seven long months, from State to State, and from one County to another. I promised Connie I'd avenge her and the baby's deaths, so now's the time to play your part. The fella standin' next to you, he ain't got no part in this feud, so I'm goin' to give him a fear warnin'. Your name's Josh, right? Well Josh, I ain't got no beef with you, but if you want to side with Tex on this one, you're goin' to the same place he is. You might want to think about that before you decide too hastily. You got five seconds. Time's out, you in or out on this one?"

Josh glances at Tex and moistens his lips with his tongue before he replies "You don't scare me, Lawman. I'm with Tex, so between the two of us, we can take you down real easy like. I'm a hell of a lot faster than you, and younger, so you've come a long way to die in a strange town. Hell, you should've chosen your casket before you decided to walk in here all high and mighty."

Tex is nervous and Josh talks too much, so Tex says "Josh! Shut the hell up, will you? It's like the lawman says; it ain't your fight, so butt out. You don't know what you're lettin' yourself in for. This lawman will shoot you before you can bat an eyelid. I've seen him do it. And to you, Jake Hudson, I ain't condonin' what I did was right, but it sure as hell was worth it."

Jake sees the look in Tex's eyes change, and the snarl on his face. His lips curl back in vicious onslaught as his hand streaks down towards his holstered six-gun. At this moment Josh decides to throw all caution to the wind and stand by Tex. The only thought in Josh's mind is to get rid of Jake and share the loot with Tex. Josh also goes for his gun.

Jake waits until Josh clears leather before he draws. Josh levels his gun and pulls back his hammer, when two bullets hit him simultaneously. The first bullet smacks into his upper torso, shattering his breastbone into splinters and imploding his heart, while the second bullet takes away part of the left side of his face. He dies without having the opportunity of seeing what and how it had happened.

Tex waits too long before he levels his gun-hand. He is shocked at the speed with which Josh has died. Tex takes aim for a kill shot; hammer cocked and finger squeezing the trigger. Jake lets him have all the pent-up rage and anger that he has had to carry with him for such a long time.

It sounds like a battleground for a couple of seconds. Jake's first bullet takes out his right eye, spraying brain matter all over the back wall and the ceiling. Tex's shot goes wide, punching a hole in the opposite wall as he staggers

backwards, already dead.

Jake shoots Tex once more while he falls, the bullet breaking all of Tex's front teeth as it enters his mouth and exits at the top of his skull. This shot throws Tex upwards and head over heels to land in a huddled-up heap on the floor. Vengeance came his way too quick and experienced for him to have it end any other way.

The fallowing day Jake saddles Jet, and after greeting Marshall Bill Paxton and his Deputies, thanking them for all their help, and wishing them all a happy future, he sets off on a fast gallop for the station in town. He will take a train and go with it as far as it can take him, or rather, as close as it can, to the town of Bitter Creek in the heart of Texas.

CHAPTER TWELVE

It's a beautiful Saturday Spring morning. Jake is in a hurry to get to the Grazing C ranch, as he can't wait to see Ronnie, and of course Buck and Cassandra as well, but especially Ronnie.

She has been the one foremost in his thoughts since he left just after Christmas. He finds that it has become more bearable to think of Connie ever since he settled the score with Tex, probably because he carried out his promise that he made to his dying wife.

Jake has also taken off his wedding ring after taking vengeance, as he thinks it will only be fair and proper towards Ronnie if he's going to court her. Fortunately he paid his debt as promised and feels that Connie has released him. She will want him to find new happiness.

That's how Connie was, so full of love, with so much passion to give and share. He once again thinks of how much luck he has been blessed with to find someone very similar in character, yet Jake knows that they are two different people.

It's as if Jet knows that it's expec-
ted of him to stretch his powerful legs more than usual, as he covers ground exceedingly fast and without much effort. "Is it perhaps Ronnie's Arabian mare that has the desired effect?, Jake wonders. The ranch house and outbuildings become visible as Jake sees the cliffs on the left of the ranch.

He puts Jet to a slow gallop and notices a figure standing on the porch from a distance, only distinguishing that it's a female. The person also sees him riding in, because suddenly there's a group of people standing around, waving at him. Getting within range of the ranch house, he sees a figure running towards him, and immediately recognizes Ronnie.

Jake doesn't give Jet much time to

slow down before he jumps out of the saddle and sweeps her up in his arms. Ronnie throws her head back and laughs with joy. Tears of happiness roll down her cheeks, as she also prayed and longed for the time to pass when Jake will return home to her. Her man is back to stay!

The End

ABOUT THE AUTHOR

CLAY CASSIDY GREW UP in a small mining town in South Africa. His love for writing started when he was still in Primary school, and captivated him throughout his entire life well into adulthood. Apart from writing, Clay also does oil painting and pencil sketching. Wildlife is his favorite genre.

Clay is also an avid reader and enjoys reading books from best-selling authors Wilbur Smith and John Grisham, as well as Louis L'Amour. A lot of research goes into the Westerns that Clay writes. Clay is very well-known for his unique and captivating style of writing Westerns.

Don't miss out!

Visit the website below and you can sign up to receive emails whenever Clay Cassidy publishes a new book. There's no charge and no obligation.

https://books2read.com/r/B-A-IZFIB-LZGID

BOOKS 2 READ

Connecting independent readers to independent writers.

Did you love *A Dish Best Served Cold*? Then you should read *The Judge*[1] by Clay Cassidy!

Random shootings occur around selected towns, leaving one dead and another seriously wounded but clinging to life. It becomes even more of a headache when Lawmen find that there are wanted posters out on the heads of the victims. It seems that someone is taking the law into their own hands after acquitted trials. The question is: Who is benefitting from these shootings, and can put a stop it before another killing is committed? A few Marshall's and a Sheriff have their work cut out for them when they take on the task of proving their suspect a wanted killer. The Lawmen find that it's not as easy as they had first anticipated, but finally manage to incarcerate him for a short while. Taking a bold opportunity, the shooter tries to make a bolt for it. In

1. https://books2read.com/u/3kO9l6

2. https://books2read.com/u/3kO9l6

his haste to escape, he is mortally wounded, and succumbs from his wounds.

Also by Clay Cassidy

Payback
The Judge
The Return
The Serial Killer
A Dozen Lawmen
Wrong Diagnosis
Rebel Cowgirl
A Dish Best Served Cold

9 798224 573691